# THE ADVENTURES OF UNCLE JEREMIAH AND FAMILY AT THE GREAT FAIR

# LECTOR HOUSE PUBLIC DOMAIN WORKS

This book is a result of an effort made by Lector House towards making a contribution to the preservation and repair of original classic literature. The original text is in the public domain in the United States of America, and possibly other countries depending upon their specific copyright laws.

In an attempt to preserve, improve and recreate the original content, certain conventional norms with regard to typographical mistakes, hyphenations, punctuations and/or other related subject matters, have been corrected upon our consideration. However, few such imperfections might not have been rectified as they were inherited and preserved from the original content to maintain the authenticity and construct, relevant to the work. We believe that this work holds historical, cultural and/or intellectual importance in the literary works community, therefore despite the oddities, we accounted the work for print as a part of our continuing effort towards preservation of literary work and our contribution towards the development of the society as a whole, driven by our beliefs.

We are grateful to our readers for putting their faith in us and accepting our imperfections with regard to preservation of the historical content. We shall strive hard to meet up to the expectations to improve further to provide an enriching reading experience.

Though, we conduct extensive research in ascertaining the status of copyright before redeveloping a version of the content, in rare cases, a classic work might be incorrectly marked as not-in-copyright. In such cases, if you are the copyright holder, then kindly contact us or write to us, and we shall get back to you with an immediate course of action.

**HAPPY READING!**

# THE ADVENTURES OF UNCLE JEREMIAH AND FAMILY AT THE GREAT FAIR

## CHARLES MCCELLAN STEVENS (QUONDAM)

ISBN: 978-93-5342-761-0

First Published:     1898

LECTOR HOUSE LLP
E-MAIL: lectorpublishing@gmail.com

"APPLES, PEARS, BANANAS, SWEET ORANGES."

# THE ADVENTURES OF UNCLE JEREMIAH AND FAMILY AT THE GREAT FAIR

## THEIR OBSERVATIONS AND TRIUMPHS

BY

## "QUONDAM"

### WITH SIXTY ILLUSTRATIONS

1898

# CONTENTS

# UNCLE JEREMIAH AND FAMILY AT THE GREAT FAIR

## CHAPTER I

### ON THE WAY

"Apples, pears, bananas, sweet oranges, five cents apiece."

"Last call for dinner in the dining car."

"Ah! this is comfortable," soliloquised Uncle Jeremiah. "All the nations of the earth contribute to our appetites, and millions are spent to transport us comfortably. Going to the World's Fair with Mary's two children, me and Sarah. Say, stranger, what time do you think we'll arrive?"

"In about two hours if we are on time, but so many people are crowding on, that I doubt if we can get there before six o'clock."

Uncle Jeremiah had addressed his question to a good-natured appearing young man just behind him who had been ostensibly reading a newspaper but really covertly watching with admiring glances Uncle Jeremiah's grand-daughter Fanny as she replaced the fragments of a lunch back into the basket. Uncle was in a communicative mood for he had just disposed of his share of one of Aunt Sarah's admirable lunches and squared himself round, as he called it, to talk with some one. Johnny was busy investigating a hole in the seat cushion and Aunt Sarah had laid her head against the window frame and was calmly viewing the flying scenery outside. The two seats turned together were occupied by Uncle Jeremiah and his family and a number of bundles and valises.

"Yes, this is a great country; and, as I have lived in it nigh onto sixty year and fit for it without seeing much of it but what I tramped over with Sherman to the sea, I concluded to take the whole world in at once by spending a month or so at the Exposition. I told Sarah we'd take Mary's two children along, for I didn't like to leave them so long with our hired help. Then they'd be company for us. Mary was our girl, but she's dead now, and so Johnny and Fanny must take her place. Me and Sarah has worked hard for many a year, and we're going to enjoy this trip ef it takes more 'n a dozen of my best Jerseys to foot the bill. We've got the best farm and Jersey herd in Park County, and I've made up my mind that we can afford it."

The stranger laid down his paper and seemed much interested in the talking farmer and his family. Fanny had stowed the lunch basket away under the seat and wearily laid her head against the back of the seat, unconscious of the respectful admiration bestowed upon her from the gentleman in conversation with her grandfather. Fanny was a very pretty miss, just reaching womanhood, and unsullied in thought or conduct by the usual desire for masculine attention. Her face was warm and full, and her light wavy hair reached her shoulders and turned up at the ends around her neck.

Johnny was too industrious in his varied investigations to notice much that was occurring about him. His keen eyes just a little turned inward gave him the appearance of shrewdness that well befitted him. He always investigated what he did not understand and the World's Fair opened a field directly in his line.

"As I was saying. I've brought along enough money to get everything we want and to enjoy life for once. I guess we can go back home then contented and have enough to talk about for the rest of our natural lives."

Uncle's new-found friend was evidently a well-to-do commercial traveler and there was something about him that won Uncle's heart at once. It was not long till Uncle had relieved his mind of all that bore on it about himself or his neighbors or his church. Uncle was a deacon and he had many original ideas about the social and religious economics of the world. The only pride he had was in his Jerseys and in Fanny, and his only ambition was to be considered a kind of Socrates by his neighbors.

The commercial traveler did not have much of a chance to talk, if he had been so inclined, but he listened with very respectful attention to the odd observations of Uncle Jeremiah. Uncle had not talked loud, but across the aisle were two young men who seemed to be listening more intently than befitted their opportunity to hear. They were faultlessly attired, and frequently exchanged observations with each other in low tones, covertly watching Uncle and his family as if they had become very interesting personages. Presently one moved to a seat a little nearer, and both apparently became absorbed in their own affairs.

"But maybe I should beg pardon, Mister. I've been talking to you all this time without introducing myself. I know it isn't just the thing, but I'm not used to sassiety. I'm Jeremiah Jones, and what is your name?"

"My name is Hezekiah Moses," said the traveling man, solemnly.

"Ah," remarked Uncle, warmly, "that sounds a right smart like a Jew name, but you don't look like a Jew. I Judge your parents were very good people."

"They were very pious people, and, of course, brought me up in the way I should go. You have quite a charming family."

"There now, I knew you had good judgments and I am glad for you to say so. Of course me and Sarah are too old to be charming and Johnny is too bad, but I take no exceptions to Fanny."

Mr. Moses thoroughly agreed with Uncle on the latter observation.

"Johnny is all right but only last week he was training one of my Jersey calves to walk a plank like he saw the lions In the circus and it fell off and broke its neck and that was not a month after it had took the prize at our county fair. And, after I had took him atween my knees and talked to him about his responsibility to his Creator, he didn't wait two days till he cut off the colt's tail so as to make it bobbed like the British and it kicked and broke its leg on the cross bar. But I do believe he's got the making of a man in him after all. I think he must be like his father, though I never seed him. You see Mary she run off to marry some man she fell in with when she went off to school, and I forbid her letting him come to see her, for you see he might be some city fortune hunter; but Mary said she knowed, and so one day when we went to town somebody drove up to our house in a buggy and I never seed her any more. I didn't think she ought to take that way to somebody I didn't know. I must have been hard hearted them days, but somehow I couldn't help it. Sarah she went to see them lots of times over in the big town across in Ohio but I couldn't leave Indiana and when Johnny was born Mary she died a senden good words to me but I couldn't help it."

The old man drew his sleeve across his eyes and continued, "You see Mary's man was all broke down, and he told Sarah to take the children and he'd go wandering around the world for a year or two. Mary was the only child we had living, and when she died I wanted to move away from where she used to play when she was a little girl, so in two years I got a good offer, and I sold out. All four of us went to see my sister in the city, and somehow didn't tell nobody where we were going, but I said I thought we would go on to California. Well, I found a stock farm in Illinois, and after a while we went back to our old home visiting, and the old neighbors told us a nice looking man had come soon after we left, and was nearly distracted to find us gone. He advertised and spent lots of money trying to find us, but at last went away broken-hearted. Then I sent Sarah right to Ohio, but Mary's man had sold his big clothing store, and some said he had gone to California, and others said one place and another, but he couldn't be found. He never came back to our old home place, nor to his old home place, for I've kept a writing ever since. Somehow he had to give us up. It broke me all down, and I've been doing all I could for the children. Fanny is getting a good education, for our town has got to be a big one now, and has a fine college in it; but I can't educate Johnny. He's always experimenting and doing damage. Howsumever, he's a great trader, and I'm going to give him a start some time. Why, I gave him a shote a month ago, and I don't believe there is a sled or a jack-knife in the hull neighborhood any more, for Johnny's got them in our garret, but the pig is gone.

"But say, Mr. Moses, you haven't said a word about your business yet, and I've been a bragging about my farm and stock for half an hour."

"Don't worry about that, Mr. Jones. I haven't got much to tell. I'm a traveling salesman for a Chicago house; and, like you, I intend to rest up for a couple of weeks and see the Fair. I am happy to say that I stand well with my firm, and I am to be taken in as the junior member soon. The head of the firm has been the friend to whom I owe all my advancement and advantage. I hope sometime to settle down into a quiet business life and enjoy a home once more. Your talk takes me back to my old Indiana home and its comforts."

"Ah, that's it, Mr. Moses, it is plain your parents have given your mind a good mold. Here, newsboy, just bring over to me and Mr. Moses two of your best five cent cigars and we'll go into the smoker and have a smoke. I don't never smoke cigars, but these are extra days, and we can afford the luxuries."

The idea seemed to amuse Mr. Moses, but he complied with the request of the friendly farmer, and, with a good-natured wink at the newsboy, took out a cigar and deftly stuck it into his pocket as he pulled out one of his own.

Uncle could find no change and without more ado took out a roll of bills from his breast pocket. The smallest bill was ten dollars but neither Mr. Moses nor the boy could change it. One of the young men across the aisle volunteered to help them out of the difficulty and counted the change into Uncle's hand. Just then the newsboy's heel struck Mr. Moses' foot sharply and there was a quick response. The change went into one of Uncle's trouser's pockets and the roll of bills into the other, when he and Mr. Moses went into the smoking car and were soon behind a cloud of smoke.

The newsboy came in presently and there were a few whispered words between him and Mr. Moses.

"Apples, pears, bananas, sweet oranges, here, five cents apiece."

There was no sale for anything eatable in the smoker just then and the boy returned to the rear cars.

"You didn't notice when the gentleman across the aisle made change for you that you got flim-flamed did you?"

"That I got what?" said Uncle.

"That you got flim-flamed. Did you count your change when that young gent gave it to you? This is a money making occasion you know and the gentry are on the make."

"Of course I counted the money. Nobody gets me that way."

"I'll bet a cigar that you haven't got over seven dollars of that ten dollar bill."

"It's a go," said Uncle as he thrust his hand into his pocket and drew out a handfull of coins. He laid his hat between his knees and counted the money into it. "Six dollars, six fifty, six seventy-five, seven, seven ten, seven fifteen."

**"UNCLE AND MR. MOSES WERE SOON BEHIND A CLOUD OF SMOKE."**

"Ah, I've not got it all out of my pocket," and Uncle's hand dived hastily into his trousers but came out empty. A look of consternation came into his face as he looked at the laughing salesman.

"Well, by Jove! I don't often lose my bets, but here, Uncle, is the cigar, for I've lost the bet. You have fifteen cents more than seven dollars. I didn't watch that gent's counting as well as I thought," and Uncle mechanically took the cigar he had so generously given to Mr. Moses a few minutes before.

"It's worth it, Mr. Moses, it's worth it. I don't begrudge the fellow for his two dollars and six bits. I feel like I ought to go in and thank him for the lesson."

"Cigars, gentlemen, best Havanas. Here, old man, is the rest uv yer change. The chappie back there wanted to kick, but he couldn't stand me look. I don't 'low no working uv me customers dat way. You see I wur next to him in a minute."

"Ah, my boy, nobody can talk to me any more about dishonorable newsboys. You keep that money. I won't have a cent of it. I'm willin' to pay fer my teaching. And here's a dollar more for you to go right back there and supply my folks with whatever eating things you've got that they want.

"You see, Mr. Moses, I know before I get through with them Arabs and Esquimaux, and Indians and African savages at Chicago I'm going to know a good deal more than I do now, and I never in my life got something for nothing, and it's too late for me to begin now."

The first suburban station of the great World's Fair city was now passed and Mr. Moses said he must return to his seat and get his grip ready for leaving the train at the next station. He gave Uncle a card on which was printed:

*William Warner*
*With The Clarendon Company*
*Wholesale Clothiers*

As he did so, he said, "Now Uncle, remember never to give a chance to pick-pockets or confidence men, watch your change and take directions only from those you know to be responsible officers; and if at any time you need a friend, don't fail to call at the office of the firm and present that card."

They returned to their seats and a frown came over Mr. Moses' face when he saw the companion of the disreputable money changer glibly talking to Aunt Sarah and Fanny. The young man bowed himself away very gracefully and went to his seat as Uncle and Mr. Moses came up.

Uncle gave Mr. Moses a hearty hand shake and God bless you as he started for the car door; but, to the astonishment of Mr. Moses Aunt Sarah and Fanny looked scornfully at him and did not in any way acknowledge his parting salute.

"Baggage, have your baggage checked?"

"Well, what a town Chicago is, anyhow. Here they've sent a man to take care of our baggage. Now, I call that all-fired hospital. Get the checks quick, Sarah."

"What hotel?" Inquired the agent.

"We're not overly pertiklar. I was talkin' some with a young fellow back here who said he was a hotel agent; but I don't mind if I go where you say. How high are your rates?"

"The Auditorium—as high as you want to go; the Northern, fourteen stories, and the Palmer, out of sight."

"Well, Mister, we don't want to go out of sight, and we don't know how high we do want to go so I guess you'd better make it fourteen stories."

The agent took the checks, gave him some tickets and passed on.

In a few minutes a uniformed young man came along and said:

"Mr. Jones, I'd like very much to book you for one of our down-town hotels.

Every convenience, gas, baths, heat, and all the modern appliances; near car lines that land you right at the Exposition gates. Best place in the city. Take you right there free of cost."

"But how high is it?"

"Only one dollar a day apiece and up as high as you want to go."

"Ah, that's it, young man. I see your mother taught you United States. You see the baggage man said fourteen stories and I didn't understand the city way of charging."

"Shall I book you?"

"Yes."

"For how long?"

"O we may stay a month. May be less."

"Say two weeks."

"All right."

"Here's your ticket with coupons. Fifty-six dollars please."

"But I haven't seen the place nor got the money's worth. I'm Deacon Jones and I always pay my debts."

"No difference, it's the rules."

"Mr. Moses said not to deal only with responsible officers. How may I be sure you are a responsible officer?"

"I'll prove it by the conductor."

The conductor was called and Uncle Jeremiah paid over his money and received his printed directions.

"Where are your baggage checks?"

"O, I've already attended to that. I'll see to that myself."

The hotel agent left and the two young men across the aisle watched with satisfaction as Uncle folded his big roll of bills and deposited them in his left trouser's pocket.

"There it is—there is the White City," some one yelled, and the people rose from their seats and looked at the most favored spot of the earth as long as it could be seen. Houses flew by, stations were passed; the placid lake, flecked with many boats, lapped the shore as with some friendly greeting. The great buildings of Chicago's business center appeared in view, and the end of their journey was near at hand.

"Chicago, all out!"

"Listen at 'em," said Uncle, "they've got our money and now they're goin' to put us off. But I guess we must be there."

**"UNCLE WAS BEING ROUGHLY HANDLED BY THE TWO MEN."**

All the people were standing as the magic words were yelled in at the front door by the brakeman. Uncle Jeremiah had not been as excited since he heard of the fall of Richmond.

With a valise, packed almost to bursting, in each hand, Uncle was preparing to do whatever he saw others do. The two young men from across the aisle had also arisen and pressed into the crowd. One was directly in front of Uncle, and the one who had made the false change had crowded himself between Uncle and Aunt Sarah. The train slowed up as the depot was reached, and all crowded toward the door. There was a low chirrup, and Uncle was being roughly jostled about by the two men, when there was a cry of "pickpockets," and the train-boy was seen swinging on to the wrist of one of the men behind Uncle and yelling "let 'er go; let 'er go."

## "UNCLE GAVE HIS CHECKS TO THE NEAREST CAB DRIVER"

The man held a wallet in his hand, but with a curse he dropped it, tore loose from the boy and rushed through the door, disappearing in the crowd.

"Here, Mister, is yer wad. Yer wants ter keep yer eye skinned fur them fellers."

Uncle warmly thanked the boy but he received this second lesson with a little less complacency than the first. Following the crowd to the outside he presented his tickets to the first hack driver he came to.

"You are pretty well supplied, aren't you dad. You have the right of way to two hotels. Which do you want?"

"Take us to the one I've paid fer."

"Which is that?"

"Well, I guess it must be the down town hotel."

"They are both down hotels. I see your baggage is booked for the Northern and I suppose you want to follow your baggage."

Without more ado all four were placed into the uncomfortably crowded hack and shortly unloaded at the Northern. An obsequious porter ushered them into the office and Uncle was astounded with a demand for twenty dollars down. "But I've paid," Uncle protested. The clerk looked at his card and assured him he was at the wrong hotel. It was now dark and Uncle concluded to pay the money and start out anew the next day. They were shown to their rooms by way of the elevator and more dead than alive, to use Aunt Sarah's expression, they flung themselves into chairs and Johnny yelled, "This is Chicago, what I've heard them talk about." They went to the windows and could not repress a shudder as they saw the street lights so far below. Aunt Sarah did not see how she could sleep so high up, but when their evening meal was done and the events of the day discussed they became as sleepy and they felt as safe as they did with the whippoorwill singing in the orchard and the hogs grunting lazily in the lane.

# CHAPTER II
## NOW FOR THE FAIR

The next morning Uncle Jeremiah was up as usual at four o'clock, chafing like a caged stable horse that could not get out to fresh air and the tempting pastures.

**"I THINK OF EARTHQUAKES EVERY TIME I LOOK OUT."**

"These confounded people won't let a fellow have his meals only at their own convenience, and the feelin' of earthquakes keeps a growing on me every time I look down out of that window. I've got to quit it." Aunt Sarah shared the same feeling, but John and Fanny decided that it was not half as high as they wanted to go before they left Chicago.

**"SAY, MISTER, I'VE PAID FARE ONCE ON THIS TARNAL MA-CHINE."**

In due time the city awoke, with a rush and a roar, to the business of the day. Uncle found the office of the boarding house syndicate a few doors away, and the family were soon safely housed in more congenial quarters.

"The Fair, Father, the Fair! When will we ever get to see the Fair? I just heard a man say that it's ten o'clock, and here we are a-fussing about in the rooms and missin' the sights."

Johnny was impatient, but not long after, the family hailed a passing street car and were on their way at last.

"Twenty cents is the fare for four of you."

The conductor rang the fares and passed on. The new scenes of the city absorbed their attention, but Uncle soon began shifting in his seat, and at last whispered to Aunt Sarah: "Say, I noticed that we went clear 'round a hull lot of blocks, and it 'pears ter me that we air goin' right backards to where we ought to go, or else this 'ere town has got two parts a blamed sight alike."

"Fare, please!"

"Say, Mister, I've paid fare once on this tarnal machine. How often do you have to pay—every once in a while?"

"Are you riding around for your health, or do you want to go somewhere?"

"That's it, Mister, exactly. I wish you'd drive this riding machine at once to the World's Fair. You've got it pasted on the front of your engine, and yet you're takin' us right back past where we got on."

"Sure, old man, you're all right, only you got on a car going the wrong way, and so went on around the loop. But you're all right now. I'll land you at the grounds; but twenty cents, please."

Twenty cents were forthcoming, and shortly the family found themselves in a maze of booths, people, streets and vehicles. It was not difficult to follow the crowd, and in a few minutes the amazed family were walking the streets of the great White City.

"Guides, World's Fair Guides!"

Uncle stopped a moment as a boy planted himself in front of him, thus calling him from the amazement of the wonderful city down to the realities of the earth.

"Guides, Mister, only twenty-five cents. This little book contains all you want to know about yonder lovely city—for the price of one small quarter you have a key to all the doors of the Fair—with this book no Columbian guard can call you down—you are free and independent of everybody with this book in your hands—it's only a quarter, remember, only twenty-five cents! Illustrated, tells you everything."

"That's it Sarah, let's buy one of these books and go home. It tells us every thing and it is illustrated. What's the use of wearing our eyes out and our feet off when we can learn it all out of this feller's book. I feel all done up on the first sight. It's too big a job fer me to undertake. I didn't calculate on such a big show."

"No, my boy. I wish I could accommodate ye but you see I ain't got no time on the grounds for reading or I'd a brought the Scriptures along. I judge it prophesied this when it spoke of signs and wonders appearing."

"Only a quarter, sir."

Uncle shook his head, but Fanny produced a quarter and took one of the books.

Near by was a booth where camp stools were to be leased.

"That is what Sarah and I will need. These young ones can walk all day." Directly Johnny had a folded camp chair in each hand and they went on following the crowd toward the Administration building. They did not go inside as most of the people did but continued on around till the basin between the Peristyle and the Administration building appeared in view. Through the columns of the Peristyle at the far end of the basin they could see the blue lake meeting the summer clouds; above them rose the dome of the Administration building till it seemed almost to pierce the clouds. They were looking upon a scene never before excelled in grandeur by the art of man. The basin was filled with gondolas gracefully plied by Venetians, launches moving both by steam and by electricity and gay sailboats of every description. In the far end of the basin was to be seen the Statue of the Republic sixty-five feet tall and standing forty feet above the water on its great stone foundation. The MacMonnies fountain was roaring with the fall of water and the heroic figures of Columbia enthroned in her triumphal barge guided by Time and heralded by Fame was outlined against the Agricultural building. From the dome of that massive structure, exhibiting the produce of our land, Diana with her drawn bow seemed to be aiming directly at them.

"Let us sit down," said Aunt, as the first wave of the wonderful vision passed over them.

"I feel more like saying, let us kneel down," said Uncle.

Fanny read from the front of the Administration building the inscriptions there about Columbus and his work.

High over the north entrance were the words:

"Columbus received from Ferdinand and Isabel, Sovereigns of Spain, a commission as Admiral of an exploring fleet, April 30, 1492."

Over the east entrance she read:

"Columbus sailed from Palos with three small vessels, Aug. 3, and landed on one of the Bahama Islands."

What common-place facts so simply stated! But they brought forth thoughts and emotions greater and greater of the wonderful consequences to mankind.

"Grandpa, you see how we have come here to learn of the world and its progress to this greatness."

"Do not speak to me now, child; I want to think," and Uncle bowed his head in his hands.

No one said anything for a few minutes, when Johnny startled them by yelling "Gorgeous! gorgeous!"

"Of course it's gorgeous," said Fanny; "but you needn't yell that way. You must not forget that you are not in our barnyard now."

Johnny subsided. He had expressed his opinion, and he was ready to move on.

Uncle arose and said: "I guess we are able to go to the next scene now, and I warn you all that the word gorgeous is as high as we will be allowed to go in expressing ourselves, no matter what we see. There has got to be a limit somewhere, and I judge that gorgeous is far enough."

"Is that the statyure of Mrs. Columbus?" asked Johnny.

"No, it's the Statue of the Republic."

"I declare I've been watching them things on that Statue of the Republic, and I really believe they're men instead of being pigeons."

"They are men," said Fanny. "No wonder that they look so little, for the book here says her forefinger is four feet long. Look at that figure on the top of the big building yonder. That Is Diana, the huntress. How tall do you think she is?"

"Nine feet," said Johnny, promptly.

"Life-size," said Uncle.

"Both wrong. The book says she is eighteen feet tall."

"Well, well, my girl, this looks like a dream, but it ain't, is it?"

There was a band-stand in front of them, and beyond that was a massive building, which Fanny found was Machinery hall. As they went on to it, Fanny read to them that it covered over twenty acres of ground and cost nearly a million and a half dollars. As they entered the door they saw one awful mass of moving machinery.

Uncle said he thought they had better sit down again and think awhile before venturing further, but Johnny urged them to come on so they could see something and do their thinking afterward.

They came to one of the doors of the power house, and Uncle sat down.

"I can't stand this pressure," he said, "I tell you I've got to sit down and look at this thing." At his left he could see into the power house nearly five hundred feet long and full from one end to the other of great boilers with the red fires glowing underneath.

On the right he looked across the hall where the great power wheel was flying and saw five hundred feet of whirling wheels, while before him there was an unobstructed view of machines but little short of a thousand feet.

They went over to the middle aisle and on past the larger machinery.

"Why Grandma, you are walking by me with your eyes shut. What's the matter?"

"Well you see, Fanny, it's too much to look at so many millions of things so I just shut my eyes and think. What's the difference if I do miss a few thousand sights."

"That's so, Fanny, we aint got used to looking yet. It looks like they had everything a working here but my old shaving horse. I wouldn't be surprised any minute to see that it had walked away from the woodshed and come over to show itself off in this here exposition. I believe I'll go over and offer them my old barlow knife. It's a score of years old but it'll bore a hole for a hame string all right yet."

They came to the place where they were making watches with the complex, automatic machinery that defies the eye to detect its movements, then there was the sewing machine with a man riding it like a bicycle and sewing carpet in strips a hundred feet long. There were knitting machines and clothing machines, and carving and molding machines, and type-setting machines, till the day was spent and they had seen only how much there was to see.

"It takes taste to paint pictures, and art to make sculpture, and mind to write books, and genius to carry on war, but I tell you, my girl," said Uncle, "that it takes brains to make machinery."

Passing through a south door they went on around Machinery hall. Some working men were passing by singly or in twos and threes. One had a wrench in one hand and a queer looking bottle in the other. The ludicrous side of the exposition now began to appear. Nothing can become so great that amusing things will not occur. They are the relaxations of mental life. One of the guards saw the man and his bottle.

"Hi, there," he shouted. The workman came to a stop, the bottle being ostensibly concealed behind his apron. "What are you bringing beer into machinery hall for?"

"I ain't got any beer," replied the workman.

"Don't tell me any such stuff. You've got a bottle under your apron."

**"THE GUARD WAS DETERMINED TO DO HIS DUTY."**

"No I haven't," and the culprit as if by accident let a portion of the bottle drop into sight. The guard made a grab for it and held it up before the seemingly confused workman.

"I'll just take you to the station-house," declared the officer. "What did you mean by telling me you had no beer?"

"It ain't beer. It's—it's—ginger ale."

The prisoner was lying. That was evident to the guard. At the same time he did not want to be placed in the position of disobeying orders against making trivial arrests. He knew by the color of the liquid it was not ginger ale. A brilliant thought came to him. He would test the beer and thus have the evidence. But here a difficulty was encountered. While the rule prohibiting employees from bringing intoxicants into the grounds is a strict one, there is a much severer regulation against guards tasting the stuff while on duty. What if his sergeant should see him with a bottle of beer to his lips! To meet this obstacle the guard led his prisoner to a secluded place behind a big packing case, and after looking fearfully around hastily uncorked the bottle and sent a huge swallow of the contents down his throat.

The result was unexpected so far as the blue coat was concerned. With a howl of anguish he dropped the bottle. Both eyes started from his head and his face turned to ashen paleness as he danced about the floor shrieking "I am poisoned." Finally he sank down with a moan and the men attracted by his cries carried him to a bench and laid him down. On the edge of the human circle about him the guard beheld the face of his prisoner. Beckoning him to his side the guard feebly said, "What was that stuff in the bottle?"

"Lard oil and naphtha"," replied the workman.

The guard was removed to the hospital, while the workmen were laughing their heartiest. In an hour the stricken officer was back at his post.

That afternoon, as the family climbed the stairs to the station on their way back to the hotel, Uncle Jeremiah was a study to the student of human nature. The size of the Exposition had dazed and awed him. He wore a neat paper collar with an old-fashioned ready-made necktie pushed under the points. The slouch hat was down over his ears, as a heavy wind was tearing across the high landing. His manner was that of one oppressed by a great sorrow. He looked at the turrets and domes and the hundreds of dancing flags and shook his head solemnly. When the people around him gabbled and pointed their fingers and piled up the same old adjectives he glanced around at them timidly and then stepped softly away where he could gaze without being interrupted. After boarding the car he stood up between the seats and held on to the railing. At each curve of the track, as new visions swung into view, he shook his head again and again, but said nothing. He had been for a good many years taking in a daily landscape of stubble-field, orchard and straight country roads. His experience had taught him that a red two-story hay press was a big building. To him the huddle of huckster stands at the county fair made a pretty lively spectacle. Then he was rushed into Chicago. With the roar of wheels still in his ears and the points of the compass hopelessly mixed, he found himself being fed into the Exposition gate with a lot of strange people. The magnitude of the great enterprise was more than any intellect could fully grasp. His mind perceived so much that was strange and new that he became as that one who saw men as trees walking. His eyes were opened to a new world. He was now a living part of the intellectual vision and prophecy of the "Dream City."

# CHAPTER III

## AROUND THE WORLD FOR TWENTY CENTS

The next day, when the "Alley L" road let them off at the station next to the electric road, they decided to ride around and view the "White City" from that elevated position. The intramural road is about three miles around, and makes the trip in seventeen minutes. It was like going around the world in that time, so much was to be seen on either side.

The four made a fine picture of age and youth gathering mental breadth from this great exhibition of human wisdom and achievement. They passed around the west end of Machinery hall and along the south side of it, then between the Agricultural annex and the stock pavilion. Here they emerged into what seemed to be the waste yard of the Exposition, debris of all kinds, beer houses, lunch rooms, hundreds of windmills flying in the breeze and heavily loaded cars, back of which could be seen bonfires of waste materials, these making a striking contrast to the white beauty and massive art on the opposite side of the car.

The queer looking Forestry building flew by, the leather exhibit was passed, and the train ran around a station not far from the Krupp gun works. They had not yet made the grand tour of the grounds, but another investment in tickets sent them back again, the way they had come, on the parallel track. When they reached the west side they looked away from the massive buildings across Stony Island avenue at the amusing medley of hotels, booths for lunches, and tents for blue snakes, sea monsters, and fat women strung along the front. Little merry-go-rounds buzzed like tops in cramped corners between pine lemonade stands and cheap shooting-galleries. Looking eastward, the eye rests with satisfaction upon the gilded satin of the Administration dome, and then it may take an observation to the westward of a flaunting placard:

*Four Tintypes*
*for Twenty-five Cents*

Back of the sandwich counters and fortune-telling booths are stored the World's Fair hotels, looking like overgrown store boxes, with holes punched in them.

The train flew on, and uncle saw little of the outside because of his interest in the strange machinery that was propelling them forward. The engineer pulled a lever and then there was a buzz and a whirr; another lever was turned, and the car would come to a standstill at some station. It was amazing to see such simple movements by one man control such unseen energy. From the farm to the Exposition grounds was as marvelous a change as from one world to another, and to the simple genius of rural work it was like going from the peaceful valley to the mysteries beyond the clouds.

Past the Esquimau village, the richly varied city of state and foreign buildings came into view. All the varieties of architectural genius from the different countries of the world appeared one after another and it was easy to imagine a flight of incredible speed all over the earth. The terminal station at the northeast was reached and uncle wanted to ride back again. In this way the panorama of the great Fair was quite well fixed in their minds when they descended from the southeast station at the entrance of Agricultural hall. For once Uncle felt at home when he walked into that paradise of grass and grain.

**"HE STOOD CHEWING A WISP OF HAY."**

"Every body but me and Sarah can scatter and we'll all meet at the far end of this house, or if not there at the south side of the Sixty-third street gate at six o'clock." Fanny and Johnny took Uncle at his word and were soon strolling among the booths, but they were more intent upon watching the maneuvers of the various types of people than of observing what the earth is able to produce out of its soil. They heard a band playing somewhere in the distance and they moved on that way.

As a curious observer of this moving world, Fanny made note of the many interesting exhibitions about her of country ignorance and enthusiasm. At one place she stopped near a tall, lank farmer, whose cowhide boots had left their massive imprint on every roadway on the grounds. He stood chewing a wisp of hay plucked from an exhibit, while he gazed in delight at the harvesters, plows and sheaves of wheat which stretched away before him in an endless vista.

"Wall, I swan," he at length confided to the dignified guard, who stood like a sign-post near the door, "this 'ere's the only thing I've seed 'minded me of hum. Bin tramping raound these 'ere grounds, scence 7 o'clock, b'gosh, an' ain't seen a blamed thing did my ole heart so much good as this show right here. By George! wish I'd a struck this buildin' fust thing I come in. Would a saved me a power of walkin'. Say, had a great show out our way a spell ago. Had a corn palace—Sioux City, you know. Be they goin' to have a corn palace at this 'ere fair?"

The guard unbent enough to guess not.

"Sho! y' don't say so. Wall, that's curious. Corn palace out to hum was the biggest show ever give out that way. And crowd! Say, I'll bet a nickel I've seed as many as hundreds of people thar in one day. In one day, reclect, all just looking at that there corn palace. Wonder these fellows didn't think of that. Would a drawd all the folks from out in our section, shore. Tell you what I don't like about this show," he went on, waxing confidential, "Too much furrin stuff here. Don't see nothing from Keokuk, Sioux City, Independence or even old Davenport. But all London and Berlin and Paris, and all them other places where they's kings and things. Ought to a give the folks here more of a show, b'gosh, same as we did out to hum. Why, they wasn't none of this statoo stuff thar, I tell you. Wasn't no picters and the like of that. What good is them picters over there, I'd like to know? Why, some on 'em, the folks ain't got a stitch of clothes on 'em, and you couldn't hang them air picters in a barn. Ought to have more of these things here—oats and wheat and seedin' machines. Them's what people want to see. And say, I was daown here below this mornin', and by gum, I seed the damdest lookin' fellows I ever seen in all my born days. They was heathen Turks, I reckon, with rags round their heads and wimmin's clo'es on all o' 'em. I was a-scared to stay there, b'gosh, and I jest lit out, I tell ye. Well, I'm goin' through here and see what you've got, but I jest tell you this is the part of this show that'll do. Yes, sir." And the rural visitor stalked away.

In less than two hours the brother and sister had reached the west doorway, but uncle and aunt were nowhere to be seen. Then they went up into the gallery to hear the musicians again. It was very evident that Agricultural hall had swallowed their grandparents for that day and the grandchildren were left to shift for themselves. It was now past noon and they were both hungry enough to welcome the first lunch counter they could find. One o'clock found them again wandering listlessly about the gallery absorbed in the sights about them.

# CHAPTER IV

## ESCORT AND BODY GUARD

"Hist, me boys," said one of a group of young men near the band-stand, who were watching the people moving about them, "Me eye has caught sight of something forbidden to all the rest of the world. You can look but you must mustn't touch. Give me your prayers boys." He sauntered away from them and came near to Fanny and Johnny as if intensely interested in all that was about him. Fanny was standing near the balustrade that was around the gallery, when the opportunity the young man was watching for soon came. Some rude man hurrying by struck her arm in such a way as to knock her hand-satchel out of her hand and it fell to the main floor far below. In an instant the young man lifted his hat, and bowing to her ran down the near flight of stairs; taking the satchel from some one near whom it had fallen, he hurried back and gave it to her with a profound bow. Seeming to recognize her all at once he made another bow and said, "Ah, pardon me but I see I have just had the honor of serving Miss Jones, whom I met on the train a few days ago." Hardly knowing just what to do, she thanked him and hesitated, but he was not slow to turn the tide in his favor and was soon chatting in such a very agreeable way about the many scenes that she soon forgot all doubts as to propriety. It was now three o'clock in the afternoon and she thought of her grandparents and what they would think; but the three hours till meeting time at 60th street gate flew by under the interesting guidance of the young man on whose card Fanny read

> *Arthur Blair*
> *Attorney*
> *Masonic Temple[S.S.]*

He explained that (S. S.) was a sign that meant "Secret Service" as he had told her before how he had been sent out to shadow Mr. Moses. They rested for awhile on one of the seats in the gallery and Mr. Blair took great interest in showing Fanny his official papers and commissions. Surely he was a very honorable and talented man.

**"HE BOWED TO HER, AND THEN RAN DOWN THE NEAR FLIGHT OF STAIRS."**

While he was pointing out his name on one of these papers, a gentleman came by who started on seeing them, as if in the most pained surprise.

"That man means her some harm," he said to himself, "and I feel as if I have no manhood if I do not undertake somehow to prevent it. But he has told her something terrible against me and I have no way to approach her."

The two arose to go and the gentleman walked not far behind.

"You do not know how it pains me, Mr. Blair, to know that such a noble look-ing young man as Mr. Moses, is a man under police surveilance. He has such an agreeable and gentlemanly appearance."

"That is true Miss Jones, but you have no idea how perfectly these criminals can assume an appearance of culture and high social standing."

Six o'clock had come swiftly and as they approached the gate Uncle and Aunt were seen sitting on their camp stools at the appointed place. The young man excused himself before reaching them and bowed himself away, but not before he had learned her address and that they came every day through the 60th street gates at nine o'clock in the morning.

"Where is Johnny?" anxiously inquired Aunt as Fanny came up alone.

For the first time Fanny seemed to realize that Johnny had not been with her for some time. She told Aunt that she had been for two or three hours with the young gentleman who had warned them on the train of Mr. Moses.

They waited and waited, growing more and more anxious about Johnny.

"Yer, yer, yer, all of you, come on out!" They knew Johnny's voice, and turned about just in time to see one of the guards holding Johnny fast by the ear as they disappeared around the corner of the wall and through the gates.

"There, you young scamp," as he gave Johnny an extra box on the ear, "let me see you trying to sneak through the gates again and you won't get off so easy."

"Well, ain't I been tellin' you fer an hour that the folks was a waitin' fer me inside and you wouldn't tell 'em fur me," and Johnny, with a disgusted shake of the head, joined the family as they came out.

"Where on earth have you been?" said Uncle, in a chiding tone of voice.

"Why, I came up to the gate about two hours ago and I seed Louis Burjois here a-peekin' through, an' I come out and we've been a-takin' in the circuses along Stony Island avenue. Say, Gran'pa, I've engaged Louis fer bodyguard fer next week when he comes back from his next run on the train. I gives him a salary of goin' wheresomever I go."

Uncle looked at the boy standing by Johnny and recognized him as the train-boy who had twice saved him from the loss of money.

"All right, Johnny," said Uncle, as he shook the train-boy's hand, "how much extra allowance will that take?"

### "LOUIS STUCK A PIN IN HER WHILE SHE WAS ASLEEP."

"Just double and a half for a regular time of it. You ought to a seen us a doin' the side-shows. You see Louis knows 'em. The fat woman is there, but not an ounce bigger than Sal Johnson at Villaville, and she's part stuffed, for Louis stuck a pin in her while she was asleep, and she never flinched. The sea monster and the man with two bootblacks at each shoe, and just as tall as the shoetops, is not much bigger than Bill Mason to hum. And the four-legged woman is no good, fer Louis he pinched one of them and it didn't kick, and the show that's got a man with his body cut off just below his head is busted. You see Louis said ef I'd pay the way in of half a dozen kids whut he picked out and instructed, he'd bust the show and prove thet the man's hed had a body. I agreed, and we all got pea-shooters at my expense, and in we went. When they drawed the curtin up my blood run cold fer there was a hed humping itself about on a table and I could see clear under the table and there was no body around there. I forgot to shoot, but Louis give the sign, and all the rest just fired the peas at his head and he howled and the head it shook awful ghastly, and then they all fired again, and the head it jest raised right up and turned the table over and shook, and the whole thing raised up and shook his fists at us and then Louis said "jiggers," and you ought to have seen us a gittin' out from under the bottom of the tent and over behind Buffalo Bill's show. They was after us, but couldn't catch us."

**"LOUIS SAID 'JIGGERS.'"**

"Johnny, Johnny," said Uncle sternly, "don't you know what I've told you about letting other people's business alone?"

"But you see, grandpa, that was a fake and you know it's everybody's duty to uproot the fakes."

"That's all right, Johnny," said Aunt, "You can uproot the things needing uprooting on the farm but you must let Chicago people uproot their own foolishness."

The sage advice was unheeded for Johnny was too full of the day's adventures with his body guard and guide.

So far they had seen little of the city of Chicago, and it was a great rest and pleasure for them to sit at the windows of their rooms or in the balcony and look out over the busy street before them or talk of the events of the day.

Uncle had gone ahead of the rest and taken his seat in a rocker at their room window.

"O grandpa, there you are," called out Fanny's clear voice as she entered the door and came quickly up to his side. "I ran ahead, and grandma and Johnny are coming."

In her face was the sweet look of guileless girlhood, and her dark hair waving back in the breeze coming through the window crowned her sweet face with the tenderest beauty. Her eyes were bright and sparkling with the interest and enthusiasm of young life. They told of a woman's soul that would one day shine out and help to make this bright world more bright and holy.

When the grandmother and Johnny joined them these four stood there with no petty jealousies or bad feeling of any description to mar their happiness as a family. The sinking sun came out from the western clouds and lit up their faces as if they all rested under God's smile of peace.

"Well, Fanny, I am closing my days on earth mighty satisfactory to me. I have been mighty alarmed about what the "Zion's Herald" said about the world's meanness, but I tell you what I have seed wasn't made by mean men. I believe I have felt more of the Lord in my soul in the last few days than I ever did before in so many years. I've seen ribbons, and threshing machines and wheat and corn for a long time but I never had any idea how much brains people had before this. I went to some of the farmer's meetings fer I felt oppressed myself and thought I was just about doing it all myself but when I come here I see I haint nowhere. I used to be afraid that the government was all a going to pieces and that my fighting for the union and that the blood of your Uncle Sam at Gettysburg was of no use but I ain't any more now afraid of the world a bustin' up. People that made the machinery that I've seen and all that have too much sense. My mind is at rest now about all such things. When I seed the big engine I didn't say nothing for I never had any use before to learn words that suited such things, so I just said nothing."

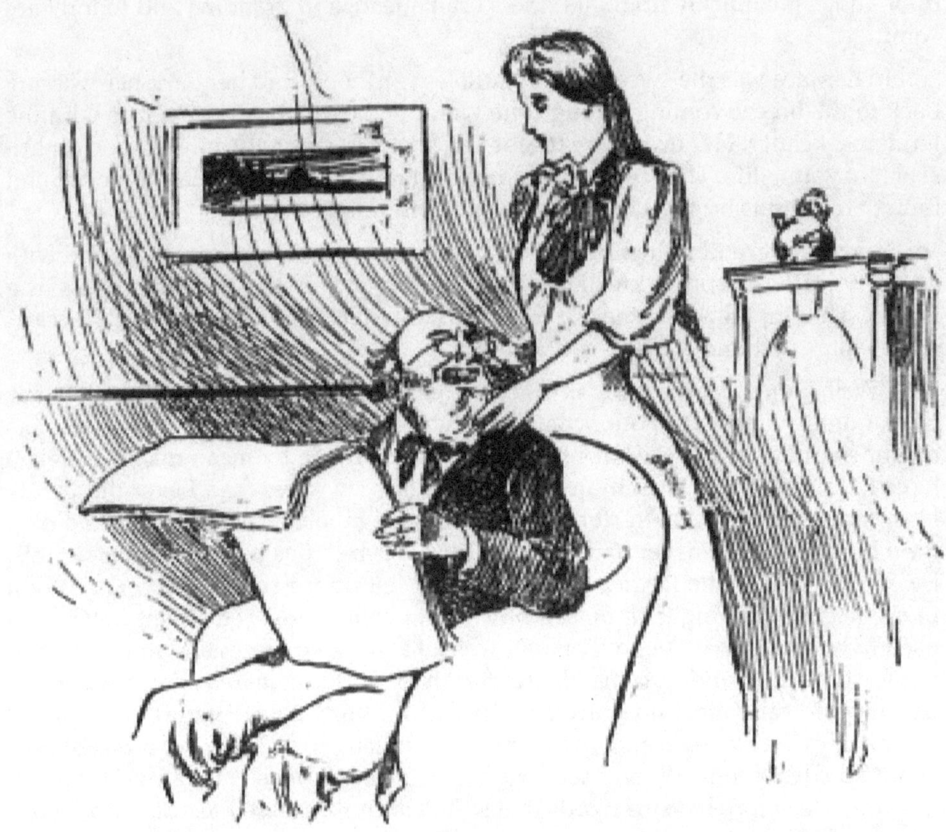

**"SHE SMOOTHED BACK THE HAIR ON HIS FOREHEAD."**

Fanny understood her grandfather's mood, and she smoothed back the hair on his forehead and gently stroked his cheeks with her hands.

"Papers, papers! 'Daily Columbian'!"

A childish voice at the door broke their reverie.

"Grandpa, you must be like city folks and read the papers."

"Here, little boy, is five cents for the morning 'Columbian' and one cent for your evening paper."

"Now, Grandpa, I want you to read. Let's see the headlines."

*"ENTHUSIASTIC THOUSANDS"*

"I was one of that crowd," said Uncle, "but it was too big to be enthusiastic over."

*"Many of the World's Distinguished People Present"*

"That may be right, Fanny, but I don't believe they are very distinguished after they get inside. I know I felt like I had just got extinguished or something."

*The Colossal Manufacturers' Exhibit Amazes the
Great Crowd of Visitors. The United States
and the Foreign Nations join in Creating
the Greatest Display in the
World's History. Shown like a
Jewel in a Frame of Light"*

"Ah, my little girl, that's my Fanny when she comes between me and the window, a jewel in a frame of light."

Fanny put her hand over his mouth and said, "Grandpa, I don't want you to scold me so unless when I deserve it."

Uncle Jeremiah having read all that interested him, turned the paper over, when his eye fell on the columns of advertisements. He had never read any of them before, and it attracted his interest at once.

"Look hyar, Johnny! Here is a position you might git if you had only done as I have teached and learnt your lesson at school." And Uncle read, slowly:

*Wanted.
—A BRIGHT, HONEST,
IN-telligent boy: good Christian;
A No. 1 writer; quick at figures, not fond of
play; never reads novels or smokes, or sets
a bad example in any way before children.
Address,* * * * * *

"Grandpa, that is a sad reminder," said Fanny, as she came up and looked over his shoulder at the paper.

"Why?"

"Because God loves a shining mark, and all those boys are dead. On their tombs should be written: 'Here lies one who lived not wisely, but too well.'"

"Tut! tut! child, how you do talk!"

"Here, father, here is the one. You know I've always wanted a parrot."

*Exchange.
—WILL EXCHANGE FINE
Parrot, good talker, for a pet monkey.
Address,* * * * * * *

"But, Fanny, where's the monkey to exchange?"

"Why, Johnny, of course. I know it would be a trade," she said, rapturously.

Johnny had come up in the meantime, and was leaning on Uncle's right shoulder. At Fanny's words he eyed her suspiciously for a moment, and then, pointing his finger at another advertisement, said: "Father, send Fanny to that place at once. Her first meal will take the people a month to digest, and that will be a big saving, for she won't have to make but one meal a month, and she will never be bothered about doing so much fixing up." The advertisement read:

*COOK WANTED.*
*—NEED NOT WASH.*
*Address, * * * * * **

Uncle crumpled the paper up in his hand and said emphatically, "O you children git out."

But they felt more like talking as they were accustomed to do of evenings at the farm. Johnny had told his adventures and Uncle and Aunt had seen wonderful things which they knew were only interesting to them. What they had seen was to them an awful revelation of what the world was doing in the various lines of work while the farmers were busy with the cares of the farm and isolated from the great industries of life where genius subdues and achieves.

"Somebody brought a heap of wool all the way from New South Wales in Australia, and I felt ashamed of myself when I seed farm products that was brought all the way from the Cape of Good Hope and I hadn't brought nothing from Villaville. We seen farmers from Japan, and China, and Ceylon. I was shocked to see how them Japanese like to have snakes and hobgoblins a crawling round their pavilions but when I seed the Americans jammed all around when there was nicer products in the other places, I just concluded that maybe after all it was our people that liked 'em too, and so made 'em set the fashion here.

"The Canadians tried to beat everything with their twenty-two thousand pound cheese. There is lots of fool extravagance in that place but I guess it was necessary to show what we farmers can do when we make up our minds."

Fanny told about meeting Mr. Blair and how interestingly he explained everything. As she looked up at her Grandma, she saw a troubled look on her face.

"It's nothing," said Grandma, "but I didn't meet young folks that way when I was a girl, and I am afeard now for you; but I've always tried to teach you right, and I know no body can make you believe I haven't teached you just right. I will trust ye. I trusted your mamma when nobody else did, and she didn't do no wrong."

Fanny went over and laid her cheek against her grandma's face and whispered: "Grandma, any body can kill me, but nobody can make me wilfully do wrong."

# CHAPTER V
## COLUMBIA AVENUE

**"THERE WAS A MEDLEY OF EXCITED VOICES."**

Several unnoteworthy days were spent by Uncle and his family in which they saw through the official buildings of the states and nations; through the Forestry building, showing the forestry wealth of the world; through the leather exhibits, showing the wonders done to the skins of beasts; all over Wooded Island, with its curiosities of Davy Crockett's cabin and the Javanese Hooden; through the clam bakes and the Casino, with the miscellaneous objects of interest about them. Uncle thought he was entering the Liberal Arts building when he walked past the guard at the southeast entrance of the Casino. He wandered into a labyrinth of side-rooms, where he heard an amazing medley of excited voices in as many different languages. They were evidently quarreling over something that displeased them very much. Presently a guard caught him by the arm.

"Are you a musician, sir?"

"Well, I used ter play a Jew's harp a leetle."

"The Casino will open again at three o'clock. You are not allowed in here."

The rest of the family had remained on the outside, suspicious of Uncle's venture. As he returned, led out in rather an undignified way by the guard, Uncle did not relish the amused looks of his family and the casual observers.

"Ah, ha," yelled Johnny in glee, "Grandpa's the first of us to get took by the cop. I'll tell everybody at Villaville about you getting led out."

From here they went on around to the north end of the greatest building on the grounds where were stored the miscellaneous educational achievements of the world.

As they entered the Manufacturers and Liberal Arts building through one of the small entrances on the north, the greatness of that more than forty-four acres of exhibits did not impress itself upon them. The first objects that met their gaze were the graphophones or phonographs. Some nickles were soon in the slots and the family for the first time listening to music coming from some where by singers unseen. Johnny had a face covered with smiles as he listened to some loud-mouthed artist singing "Throw him down McClosky." Between each verse Johnny told the boy who stood in open-mouthed wonder near him that the "feller is a singer from way back." He could not realize that he was not in a concert hall and that all standing about were not hearing what he heard. When the music ceased and he withdrew the tubes from his ears he said to the boy, "Wasn't that out of sight?"

**"THEY LISTENED TO MELODIES BY MUSICIANS UNSEEN, AND FROM SOMEWHERE UNKNOWN."**

"Sure, and out of my hearing too, but I guess I got a nickle to try it on," and his nickle disappeared in the slot and the unwearied singer hid away in the machine told again his story of the great fight.

When Uncle took the tubes from his ears his eyes were full of tears.

"Why, Grandpa, what's the matter?" asked Fanny who had just listened to some selection by the Marine band.

"Well, you see, I heard something that I used to hear long time ago, and I couldn't tell just who was a singin' it to me. It was some woman, though, and I let myself think it was somebody else, and I was a thankin' God for lettin' me hear her once more. I thought it was Mary singin' "Old Folks at Home" for me, jest like she used to, and I thought for a while that she had come back to me. I wanted to talk to her, and it hurt me when I seed that I couldn't."

There was a stairway near by, and Fanny suggested that they should first go above. They came to the place where they could look out into the main floor. They were near the great clock tower just as the chimes began to peal forth their weird melodies.

"What's that?" cried Aunt, in awe-struck tones.

"It's the chime of the bells," cried Fanny, in delight, "listen! listen!"

Clear and plain through the vast building and to the streets on the outside came the slow measured notes of that nation-thrilling air, "My Country, 'tis of Thee."

All stood entranced before a scene never before reached by human means. When the chimes were done, Uncle said: "Let us go down to the main floor. I want to walk from end to tother of that aisle."

Johnny held in each hand a camp-stool for Uncle and Aunt, and he arranged the stools for them to sit awhile before that wonderful scene. Not long after, they were marching down that aisle called Columbia avenue. They felt themselves every inch as citizens of a great republic. It is not a very long thoroughfare—only a third of a mile—but they were two hours on the way. Uncle was a common, every-day American citizen when he started. At each step it seemed to him he swelled in his own estimation. At the clock tower he was proud enough to ascend that structure and make a Fourth of July speech. At the end of his walk he wanted to wear an eagle on his hat and shout till his throat should be stiff. It was not solely as an American that he was filled with exultation but as a member of the human race. He was lifted up with pride in the achievements of his fellow-man and in satisfaction that his own country was the host of such a splendid company.

Columbia avenue is the broad thoroughfare which traverses the center of the greatest building that ever was. It runs through the Manufactures and Liberal Arts building from the grand court to the plaza at the northern end. A walk down this thoroughfare is like a tour of the world in sixty minutes. Though, if you are to do it in sixty minutes, you must fifty times repress an impulse to linger beside some new marvel in the handiwork of man and go marching on. You cannot beat the record in a trip around the world and stop and see all the grand cathedrals and picturesque ruins and beautiful women and inviting galleries of art.

Columbia avenue is a picture never to be surpassed. It is a cleanly and an attractive thoroughfare for the world of tourists who throng the way. The path is no longer littered with lumber and boxes and kegs of paints. The horizon—for this vast enclosure has its horizon—is no more filled with a fine, white mist rising from the efforts of workmen to push and chisel blocks of staff into their appropriate places. It is a colossal field of process and a panorama of result. The world can not produce a more noble and inspiring place. It is the avenue down which the man on whom fate has fallen and whose steps in this world are few should choose to expend the last remaining atoms of his strength.

Uncle, as an American citizen, came in pride and exultation into the avenue from the central court. He had not been there before. The first thing he did was to stand fully five minutes gazing at the immensity of the enclosure trying to comprehend it, instinctively but vainly seeking adjectives with which to characterize it, and finally giving it all up, as a man gives up trying to measure the ocean or count the stars, conceding it to be too vast and wonderful for the range alike of his vision and his mind. No one told him which way to go, but away over his head, he couldn't guess how many hundred feet, was a line of pendent stars and stripes extending so far in a perspective of red and white that he could not see the fartherest. For aught he knew to the contrary the line led away to the sunny South. But knowing that where the stars and stripes led the way, he could go as he had done in the years of war, he passed on through a maze of wonders greater than even a Solomon could dream.

Not a word had been spoken for some time. Fanny had stopped at a millinery booth.

"Well, now come on Fanny, you wouldn't let me look at them harrows to my heart's content so come on, for you might get ideas into your head that would cost me lots of money and you know these times are expensive enough anyhow."

At the south end of the hall they ascended to the galleries again and soon, came past the educational exhibits that cover every department of human training. There was a booth of educational temperance. Here they read:

> *The Star of Hope*
> *of the Temperance Reform*
> *stands over the*
> *School House*

These letters were on a banner of beautifully wrought silk, and near by was a map of the United States, with seven states distinguished from the rest by being in the darkest black.

"Those states," explained the ladies in charge, "have no school legislation for teaching temperance."

"Yes," soliloquized Uncle, "the school house, the pulpit and the press, are the three forces of freedom and progress in our welfare, but our lives and our natures are not alone molded by these. The fathers and mothers in the home holds greater destinies for the world than all the rest of the forces of the earth together." Then they went through a modeling department. Uncle could not see any use of these things.

"Now, Fanny, I'm tired of these mixing wax and realities together. Here's a man's head four feet across in this glass case. What does it mean?"

"O, that's just an enlarged figure to show the anatomy."

"Well, I didn't come here to see 'natomy, so let's pass on and leave it to other folks that like sich."

Just then some good country people came up and they were almost wild for knowledge as to where the Exposition people dug up that awful giant, and as to how long he lived before the flood, and if it might not be Goliah. Fanny could not stand such an error, and she pointed out to the little girl the card below explaining what the figure intended to show.

They went on past states and foreign countries, and booth after booth of books and papers of the great publishing companies.

"Come here, come this way, all of ye!"

Johnny was wildly motioning to his folks, who had stopped to examine some books in a booth near the north end of the Liberal Arts hall. As they came up to him, he said: "Say, you remember the Century plant, don't you, down in the Horticultural hall, wot's jest bloomed? Well, I've found a Century company, an' I want Fanny to go in thar an' ask the gurl wot hes charge if we kin see it bloomin'."

"They are the people who publish so much about the war and about Lincoln. Let us go in and I'll take some notes about what they have."

Fanny took out her pencil and notebook as they approached the entrance of the booth. All went in together, and the lady in charge, seeing Fanny with a notebook in her hand, came over to her from the opposite side of the room with a rush that almost took the young observer's breath away.

"Are you a reporter, Miss?"

"No, no," said Fanny.

"Oh! Just taking notes for your own amusement."

"Well, not exactly that. I may use them some time."

Fanny had in mind the things she would have to tell to her less fortunate friends at home.

"O I see, going to weave them into a book or a lecture. Just come this way;" and, followed by Johnny, Uncle and Aunt, Fanny went the rounds of the place listening attentively to the interesting talk of the lady in charge as she explained the processes in detail of making a great magazine, the evolution of the English dictionary and of dictionary making in all its phases. She showed them many interesting relics and among them the original letters and documents of the company's great war articles and their life of the martyred president. The lady never had more interested listeners or people more grateful for the trouble she had taken to instruct them.

**"UNCLE DID NOT RECOGNIZE HIM."**

"No, don't go till you have registered."

Fanny went over and registered for all of them and Uncle went away feeling as if he now had a literary education and could write anything from a war article to a dictionary.

They passed on down and out of the building more impressed than ever concerning the greatness of the world. Aunt rarely said much but now she remarked that she loved their farm and their Jerseys more than ever but she could see that God's mercies and blessings did not rest alone on them and their neighbors. There was indeed a world beyond what she had ever seen or been able to dream.

As they passed on to the gate a family evidently from off the farm passed them.

The eyes of Uncle and the farmer happened to meet and the farmer nodded to him.

"Now look at that," exclaimed Uncle. "How cityfied I'm getting. I didn't nod to that feller. The fust few days I was here I nodded to everybody who looked at me but when they stared back at me like I was an idiot, I quit."

As they came by the Administration building a gentleman passed near them and politely lifted his hat. Without response Aunt and Fanny went on but Uncle grasped the gentleman by the hand and said, "Mr. Moses, I am so glad to see you. I ain't been tuck up yet by the perlice nor lost any money but I guess I would if you hadn't give me such good advice."

"Uncle, I must tell you that my name is Warner, as you have it on my card and not Moses. I told you that name just for a joke because I didn't expect to see you again and you know we don't often tell our names and business to people we meet on the trains."

Uncle was very much troubled. He could not see any joke in a false name being given. He remembered then that Fanny said a young man on the train was shadowing Mr. Moses, and this false name made it look bad for Mr. Warner.

"Well Mr. Warner I am sorry you deceived me for I liked you very much and I aimed to call on you, but maybe I hadn't orter not."

Without another ward Uncle went on to join his waiting family, sadly shaking his head as he thought of the misplaced confidence he had bestowed.

"There," said Mr. Warner, "I have estranged the good opinion of the old man and in his mind made the words of the confidence man seem true. But somehow I feel sure that I shall meet her in a different way."

As he looked after her he said, "There goes the dearest girl on earth to me."

**"HE LOOKED AROUND AFTER HER."**

It was arranged that the next day the old people should rest at their hotel all day and at two o'clock Fanny would go to one of the big retail stores to do some needful shopping with Johnny as an escort.

# CHAPTER VI

## DANGERS OF THE GREAT CITY

Johnny was listlessly walking along in front of Dearborn Station, on Polk street, when he saw some fine looking apples on one of the fruit stands. Instantly the old orchard at home came into his mind, and with it a hunger for apples that could not be downed. Fishing up a dime from his pocket, it was not long till two apples were his, one of them undergoing a carving that only a country boy hungry for apples could perform. As he turned the corner he passed a number of bootblacks tossing pennies to the edge of the curbing, the one lodging his penny nearest the edge winning all the other pennies. Johnny watched them long enough to understand their gambling game and then moved on.

"Hi ther, kids," said one, "watch me git a free lunch."

He came quickly up behind the unsuspecting boy and struck one of the apples out of his hand. But before he could pick it up, Johnny gave him a shove that sent him sprawling in the mud. Johnny stooped to regain his apple, but half a dozen of the other boys ran up and began striking him from all sides. His knife was open in his hand, and some one struck him a blow on the hand that knocked the knife into the gutter. Warding off the uncomfortable blows as fast as he could, he ran to get his knife. In an instant he was tripped down upon his face with half a dozen boys cuffing him about the head and shoulders.

"What you skates a-doin' there. Come off now; let a feller have a show!"

The boys were thrust back, and Johnny scrambled to his feet.

"Hello! If it ain't de kid wot's got de purty sister an' helped me to pepper de fake on Stony Island avenoo. Bin a-crapin', have ye, an' them fellers wuz a-doing ye up." It was the train-boy who had been of such service to Johnny's grandfather as they came into the city.

## "BEEN A CRAPIN', HAVE YE!"

Johnny explained how it all happened, and they went away from the crowd. Johnny's clothes were soiled and his knife and apples were gone, but he was glad to get out of such a rough crowd.

"Where wuz ye goin'?"

"I've got an hour yet, when I am to meet Fanny at the north entrance to the store she's tradin' at. I couldn't stand taggin' after her, so she let me go."

Johnny had wandered from the store into the neighborhood of one of the most disreputable places in the city. He and his friend were coming up the street when the train-boy exclaimed: "Hi, thar, wot's yer sis doin' on dis devilish street wid dat thief yonder?"

Johnny looked where the boy was pointing, and, sure enough, Johnny saw his sister being escorted along the street by Mr. Blair, who had spoken to them of Mr. Moses on the train, and who had been with Fanny one day at the Fair.

"Why, ain't he all right," said John.

"Nary all right. Wusn't he helping to rob your grandad as he was a coming out of the train, and did'nt I nab his pal with the wad of stuff in his hand? He works with the feller what give yer old dad the short change."

Johnny would have started on a run after his sister but Louis said, "Hold on pard, I'm a running this. Ef your sis is all right, that feller is liable to git to travel over the road fer it. I've got it in fer that feller and you see if I don't git him pulled. I tell you if he gits your sis into one of them houses, she'll never come out alive fer she'll kill herself."

Johnny was white with fright but Louis laid his hand on Johnny's shoulder and said: "Now you watch the show."

A policeman was at the next corner and Louis walked up to him with the air of one who had a most important communication to make.

"Me name is Louis Burjois, and dis is de brudder of dat gal wot you see walkin' over dere. She is an innercent gal, which dat feller is a-tollin' of her off. He's a pickpocket, and I'm one wot kin swear to it. We want him arrested an' jugged. We'll see to all de responsibility."

"Ah, you Arabs don't take me in that way. Git out. The gal knows her biz."

By this time Louis saw that the confidence man had stopped at one of the most prepossessing houses on the street. It was also one of the vilest and most dangerous places in the city. The door-bell had been rung, and there was not a moment to lose.

**"SHE'S AN INNERCENT GIRL WHAT'S A GITTIN' TOLLED OFF."**

"For God's sake run and yell!" and he gave Johnny a push in their direction, which was all he needed to send him flying up the street yelling and waving his hat and calling "Fanny! Fanny! Fanny!" like a boy gone mad.

The door had opened and Fanny was about to step inside, when she heard her name called. She turned around, but the young man crowded up behind her.

"Who is calling me?" she said. "It must be Johnny. Yes, it's his voice."

"No, it's only a bootblack," her companion said, harshly and excitedly.

"I know its Johnny," and she dodged by him out of the door. He tried to catch her by the arm, but, missing that, seized her dress, nearly tearing it off of her waist. At this moment Johnny dashed up, and, throwing his arms around her, cried: "O Fanny! Fanny! come quick! come away! don't wait a minute!" and he fairly dragged her to the sidewalk.

The young man disappeared through the door but not before he saw Louis come running up and shaking his fist at him yelling at the top of his voice, "O you horrible old cheese, I'll get your mug behind the bars some of these days in spite of yourself."

The policeman was placidly watching the scene, but concluding at last that something unusual was happening he came up and went into the house. A few minutes after he came out alone and walked measuredly on toward the end of his beat.

Fanny in the meantime had pinned her dress and was walking away with the two boys. She was not less excited than they were.

"What is the matter? I can't think. What has happened; there must be something awfully wrong."

"Well, you see, miss, that feller is the pall of the man what tried to rob your grandad and he was a taking of you to one of the worstestes places in Chicago."

"Why he showed me his detective star and also papers and business cards the other day at the Fair. I met him this time in the store. While we were talking there he showed me a blue book which he said was a list of the best society of Chicago, and he showed me his name and his sisters'. I didn't know anything how to trade at the big stores and he said it would please him so much to take me and introduce me to his mother and sisters, who lived only three or four blocks away, and one of his sisters would come back with me and I could do my trading in half the time and to so much better advantage. He talked so nicely that I didn't see how I could refuse to go."

"That's the chap exactly. He's a bad man, and I'm a going to run him in yet."

Louis gave a self satisfied toss of the head, clinched his fists and said, "Its lucky, awful lucky that I seed ye." Fanny shuddered and she whispered a fervent prayer of thankfulness.

They had now arrived at the store and Louis acted as ready escort to the various booths where Fanny desired to trade.

"Don't you forgit that you have to meet me at the Sixtieth street gate at nine o'clock next Monday morning for to be my body guard the whole week and I think I can get our grandpa to throw in about two dollars a day for ye for general services. Anyhow, I don't see how any of us can feel safe any more without you being around. I expect if you come out to our farm, I'd save your life about a dozen times a day for the first week, you'd need me around pretty bad for the first month."

"It's very glad I am that I struck you," said Louis, "for my dad got killed cause he stuck by his engine and I have to help the folks so much that I couldn't get into the Fair only by scheming somehow, and I might not hit the combination."

Fanny and Johnny, still bewildered over their adventures, now took a cable car and in a little while were telling their astonished grandparents about their day's experiences and Fanny's wonderful escape from the confidence man. Uncle could not remember Mr. Blair, but it was a good occasion for one of his impressive lectures on the providence of God.

It was an evening for the electric display at the grounds and at eight o'clock they were seated near the statue of the Republic on the south side of the basin waiting to see the crowning achievement of modern intellect.

No wonder that the papers of the next morning spoke of the "White City in a blaze of glory," and that "thousands viewed the sight, entranced with the marvelous exhibition." It was a sight to inspire the writers of the day, and of all the descriptions that Fanny culled none were more appropriate for recalling the memories of what she saw, and to record what she had experienced, than the reportorial sketches of this night. The hour approached for the most wonderful illumination since God said: "Let there be light."

Slowly night came on, and slowly night was turned back into day. A few stars came out and shone for a little while, and then disappeared from man because of the blaze of light he was in.

To the north and west a heavy pall of smoke brooded over the city. Above it a broad band of gorgeous crimson, shot with purple and yellow, marked the dying glories of the day. Overhead scattered clouds floated against a gray sky, and through them yellow stars were shining. Looking down into the grand basin the white walls of the palaces which bound it loomed gray and ghostly. On the southern horizon the chimneys of a blast furnace belched their red flames high into the darkness.

One by one white globes of light glittered about the graceful sweep of the basin. They cast deep black shadows on the walls behind them, and threw burnished, rippling ribbons over the dark water below. The broad avenue leading to the north between the Mines and Mining and the Electricity buildings grew brilliant on either side. At its far northern end a clump of tangled shrubbery lay in heavy shadow, and still beyond, stretching away for miles, a hundred thousand scattered yellow sparks told that the great city was awake. Far off on the dark lagoon, men were singing, and the echo of their voices rose faintly through the silence.

Suddenly a single beam of yellow light, like a falling star, flickered and grew bright on the high dome of the Administration building. Then lines of fire ran down its splendid sweep, and outlined in flame it stood out in splendor against the night. About its base circled a wheel of light, while above a hundred torches flared into the darkness. Within the great buildings about the basin electric coronas were ablaze and the giant pillars of the colonnades loomed white against the shadows. From their caps huge figures of the arts of peace leaned out over the black abyss beneath. Along the top of the peristyle flickered a yellow ribbon of flame, and above, dim and gray against the sky, senators and heathen gods look down upon the glory.

Between these lay the dark waters of the basin, seamed with faint, waving bars of light. Over them, like long black shadows, graceful gondolas slipped in silence, and electric launches with their fiery eyes crept across the vista.

From the roof of Music hall a wide pyramid of fierce white light was thrown upon the Administration dome. Its blazonry of yellow died away, and under the new glare the delicate, lace-like tracery of gold and white was brought into strong relief. From the roofs of the buildings of Manufactures and Agriculture twin search-lights beat down upon the MacMonnies fountain. Behind it the plaza was black with men, and its pure white figures shone as if carved from Parian marble.

Then the light was changed, and in a glory of crimson the ship Columbia, with its white-armed rowers, sailed on before the people. From his high pillar on either side, Neptune, leaning on his trident, looked down serenely. The search-lights swept the horizon, and for a moment graceful Diana loomed against the sky like a figure suspended in midair. At the east end of the basin the Golden Republic glittered against the night, lifting her golden eagle high above the crowd. Smoke from a passing engine rose about the dome of the Administration building, and its fiery outlines flickered and grew faint. The triumphant goddess seated high on the galley in the central fountain was bathed in a glory of green fire, and then yellow, changing again to its spotless white.

Under the great central entrance to Electricity building stood all the while the figure of an old-time Quaker. His eyes looked upward, and he held in his hand the feeble instrument which made possible the glories of this night. Franklin, with his kite, looked out upon the consummation of what he dreamt of when he drew lightning from the summer cloud. For two hours the "White City" blossomed in new beauty. The great basin was bathed in a flood of fairy moonlight. Outside the peristyle the lake beat its monotone against the walls. On the plaza the great orchestra of more than 100 men played patriotic music, and the people were filled and lifted with the spirit of the night.

The search light was a great surprise. It went dancing along the fronts of opposite buildings, climbed up the towers and brought out golden Diana. It flashed against the statue of the Republic, and kept it for a full minute resplendent as though carved from a block of flame and then flickered away, leaving the great figure in twilight uncertainty. After a time three irregular splashes of light were playing hide-and-seek along the basin and up the fronts of the big building. The lights changed their colors. Sometimes they were green and again they were blue or red.

While several thousand people were admiring this picture, a rocket of light shone out from one of the high corners of the agriculture building and flooded the MacMonnies fountain in a whiteness which made all the other light seem dim and lifeless. Under its focus the golden caravels and the draped figures showed strange contrasts of chalky pallor and deep shade. Only a moment later a second bar of light leaped out from a sky-high nook of the Manufactures building and swept the surface of the basin. It struck a moving gondola, and in a flash showed the gay Venetians bending to their long oars, the bright colors of the boat and the muffled forms of the passengers.

Johnny had left the others absorbed in their trance of delight. He sought other sights. Directly he came to the Electricity building, with its marvels of light. It burst on his childish mind, seeking for novelties, as greater than the scenes outside. It was something that Fanny and Uncle and Aunt must see. He ran in the greatest haste to bring them. When they came in, Johnny showed them where to sit to see the great illumination in the center of the building. It was then quite dark about them, but Johnny knew the marvelous sight he had said was there would soon appear.

Four rows of colored bulbs containing incandescent lights and placed on zig-zag frame works forty feet long in different directions are about a pillar around which are twined strings of two thousand electric bulbs of red, white and blue. The pillar is covered with bits of reflecting colored glass, thus making a magic intermingling of lights that almost rival the lightning in startling brilliancy and produce a pillar of fire scarcely surpassed even by that one which led the Israelites across the sea.

When the illumination came the weird ingenuity of the electric magicians struck Aunt Sarah with a sublimity almost more than she could endure. As the flashes of light struck out about the pillar and the ball of fire fell as if dropped from some creating hand she screamed, "O my God, what blasphemy is this that men have achieved. Can they snatch the fire from heaven and make the lightening a plaything?"

She sank upon a chair and gazed stupefied for some minutes at the awful scene. Then as they passed on she said, "I have seen the wonderful machinery great and small. I have seen the old relics which they say are the remains of men's hopes long gone by, but when man can take the light that comes out from the storms and put it up for show, it seems to me that I am seeing forbidden things and that the skill of men has gone too far."

## "THE LIGHT SHOT ACROSS THE SKY."

At the next flash from the tower there was a shriek and a crowd began to gather about a man just across the hall. The cry came from a man who could receive the terrible grandeur but he did not have the strength of mind to sustain it.

He was gazing upon the incandescent globe-studded column, as in a trance, and again one of the electricians turned on the current and the shaft changed to living fire. The man seemed horrified by the unearthly beauty of the spectacle. It continued but a minute, when the current was turned off and the blinding light disappeared almost as suddenly as it had come.

A bystander whose attention happened to be directed toward him says that he stood gazing at the column for fully three minutes after the light had been turned off and that his countenance betrayed overwhelming bewilderment. Once or twice he raised a hand and drew it across his forehead. Then he was seen to press his temples with both palms, all the while gazing in an awe-stricken way at the great pillar. The attention of several visitors was attracted to the farmer, and one of them stepped to his side to inquire if anything was wrong with him. As the gentleman reached his side the latter threw his arms upward and, with a shriek that started the echoes, fell forward upon his face. Two or three guards rushed to the prostrate man's assistance, but before they reached his side he leaped to his feet and, screaming at the top of his voice, ran through the aisle toward the entrance facing the lagoon.

In a moment all was excitement, and the great crowd of visitors, becoming panic-stricken, ran in a dozen different directions or hid behind exhibits. The madman, pursued by a half-dozen guards, dashed down a side aisle and, leaping over boxes and machines, made a complete circuit of the General Electric company's exhibit and then paused again before the central column. Two guards seized him, but he threw them off as though they had been infants and again he started on a wild hurdle race through the building. He had not gone far when he tripped and fell, and in a moment three bluecoats were upon him.

Struggling and shrieking, the poor man was half led, half carried, to the north entrance of the building, where was waiting a patrol wagon. It required the combined strength of five guards to get the unfortunate man into the patrol wagon. Throughout the short drive to the patrol barn the prisoner fought like a wild animal and the officers had their hands full in keeping him aboard. When brought before the sergeant the prisoner became exceedingly quiet and spoke rationally while giving his name and address.

One of the guards then began to detail the offense of the prisoner. The recital had but just begun when the man became greatly excited and began screaming once more. The sergeant placed his hand in a kindly way upon his shoulder and gently forced him into a chair. The man grew quiet again and listened to the guard relate the story of the arrest without interruption. When the officer had finished the man arose and, walking up to the sergeant, said:

"Don't harm me, I didn't put all those bottles there. I'll tell you how it was. Somebody has stuck those bottles on that post and covered them up with a white cloth. When they raised the cloth the bottles turned to fire. I am not to blame. I don't know how those bottles came there. There are millions of them. They were all right at first, but the devils poured red fire into them. Don't hurt me. I had nothing to do with it."

The sergeant talked kindly to the man, and when he was quieted led him to the hospital, where a doctor attended to him. Here he entered into a long description of the pillar of "bottles," by which he evidently meant the incandescent globes. The doctor gave his patient a quieting potion, and in a short time he fell into a sleep. When he awoke from his sleep he was quiet, but his mind still dwelt on the pillar of "bottles," and he insisted on repeating his version of the affair to all the doctors. In the evening a carriage took the patient away, supposedly to the detention hospital.

# CHAPTER VII
## ON BOARD THE "ILLINOIS"

"Now for the battleship," said Johnny, "that's what I want to see." As they came on board the brick ship, the first words they heard were quite nautical.

"It's eight bells."

"Aye, aye, sir!"

The bos'un, or whoever it was that received the order from the Lieutenant, climbed up and tapped out eight strokes on the big brass bell. About twenty people, with lunch baskets and camp-chairs, ran after him and watched the performance.

"What's that for?" asked a young woman.

"That tells the time of day," answered her escort.

"But it's after 12 o'clock by my watch and he struck it only eight times."

"Well, they—ah—they have a system of their own. It's very complicated."

"Look at that crooked thing there," said one of the visitors, pointing to the air-tube leading to the stoker. "Is that their foghorn I've heerd about?"

"They don't need no foghorns on warships. I jedge it's a shootin'-iron of some kind or other, maybe a gattlin' gun what jest blows the shot out. You see it's pointin' out like at an enemy."

An elderly woman stepped up to the Lieutenant and said: "I'd like mighty well to see some of the Gatling guns."

"Yes, ma'am, you will find them at the foretop."

"How's that?"

"At the turret in the fore-top."

**"MAYBE ITS A FOG HORN, OR A GATLING GUN."**

"Do you mean up in the little round cupola?"

"Cupola, great heavens," murmured the officer under his breath. Then he called a marine and had him show the woman to the fore-top. It is the experience of a lifetime for a naval officer who has cruised in the Mediterranean and rocked over the high waves of the south Atlantic to be placed in command of a brick battleship, which rests peacefully alongside a little pier and is boarded by hundreds of reckless sight-seers every day. The conning towers are of sheet-iron and some of the formidable guns are simply painted wood. It is said that if anything larger than a six-inch gun should be fired from the deck of the mimic battleship the recoil would upset the masonry and jolt the whole structure into a shapeless mass.

Below the water line the Illinois is a hollow mockery, but the two decks, the turrets and the heavy battery are made so realistic that any one who had not seen the brick laid and the plating put on might suppose it was a real war vessel that had stranded well in toward the beach. As a matter of fact, about one-third of the visitors are deceived, which fact may be vouched for by any one of the marines parading the deck. A man who looked as though he read the newspapers, called a sergeant of marines "Cap," and remarked that it was a very fine vessel.

"Yes, indeed, sir," replied the sergeant.

"She'll be here all summer, will she?"

"Oh, yes."

"Did this boat take part in the review at New York?"

"No, sir; this battleship is stuck fast here. It is a shell of brick, built up from a stone foundation, and is intended to represent a model battleship."

"You don't tell me. Made of brick, eh?" Uncle, listening to the talk, shared the countryman's disgust.

"There, Fanny, how do you excuse them for that piece of mockery? Everybody getting fooled as if they were in a cheap dime show. It's too bad the government should be a partner to sich deceptions. And then just hear them fellows making fun o' the likes o' us. It's a shame. Of course we hev to ask questions when they use all the art in the world to make deceiving things and then make fun if they do such good work as to fool us. We don't know any more about their work than they do about our farm. I guess they couldn't tell a Jersey from a short-horn, nor a header from a clover-huller."

One of the sailors was telling of the questions asked by the public. Some person asked him if the gulls flying around the ship were sea-gulls, and whether they had been brought on especially for the Fair. Another asked why the guns were plugged up at the end with pieces of wood. A marine said the plugs of wood made them air-tight, so that they wouldn't sink if they fell overboard. Maybe the man believed it. He didn't say anything.

From sight-seeing at the ship they came over to the Fisheries building.

The throng of visitors here at first detracted their sight from the wall of fish and wonders of the sea around them.

"Oh," said Aunt when she looked about, "I nearly have to gasp to make sure I'm not at the bottom of the sea. Just look at them fish swimming around on both sides of you."

"Well I feel sorry for these poor fish, they look so tired," said Fanny, "but it's very evident they can't keep lively all the time."

One of the big scaly-backed tarpons in the fountain was fanning his tail and moving slowly through the water. On the railing at the edge of the pool sat a tired man with a baby hanging over his arm. If the tarpon had stuck his nose out of the water he could have grabbed the man by the coat-tail and pulled him backward. The mother was standing a few feet away. She turned around and saw two beady eyes shining up through the water.

"Hold tight to that child," she said. "If you ever drop him that big pike would gobble him right up."

"He don't eat babies," replied the husband, calmly. "Besides, it ain't a pike; it's a sturgeon."

"Well, he looks awful mean, anyway." The husband, merely to reassure her, moved a few feet further along and let the baby lie over his shoulder and watch the little fish chase one another. The aisles were crowded full of people, who had found that a visit to the east end of the Fisheries building was almost as good as a dive to the bottom of the ocean.

It is in this place where you may stand with coral reefs and ring-tailed shells on either side and watch strange fish with spikes on their backs open their mouths and gape until each one looks like the letter O. The sea turtles stand on their heads and wave yellow flippers at the wide-eyed crowd, and a devil crab makes all the women shiver and pull the children away from the glass. In one aquarium there are so many catfish that they make the water cloudy.

In front of one of the cases there was a learned discussion. The label simply said "Anemone." On the rocks and shells were some things shaped like stars and mushrooms, except that they were moss-colored and had whiskers floating out in the water. "Annymone, what the dickens are they?" asked a man with a linen duster.

"Some kind of sea-weed, I believe," said an elderly gentleman in a patronizing manner.

"No, they ain't they're animals, broke in a third.

"But, sir, they are stuck fast there and can't move," said the elderly gentleman.

"I know that but they reach out with those whiskers and grab stuff and feed themselves that way."

"Well, that's the first time I ever heard of anything feedin' itself with its whis-kers."

One of the young women looked at the sheepshead aquarium and murmured: "What long bills they have." Her escort smiled in a knowing way and said: "That is not a bill; that is a proboscis, I believe. I wish I had a hook and line."

A Columbian guard said he was tired of hearing the same old jokes, for nearly every young man who came in with a girl said: "When I come back here I'll bring a hook and line."

They finished the day here, and wearied with the noise and tumult of the streets were glad to find rest in their rooms when evening came.

**"NEXT TIME I'LL BRING A HOOK AND LINE."**

The sweetness of this rural family was nowhere better to be seen than when they were resting at home in the evening after the fatiguing experiences of the day.

"Grandpa," said Fanny, when they were comfortably at rest, "I can't help but get angry at the women as I walk about, for I do see them do so much foolishness. Why, to-day I saw one crazy for souvenirs, and I believe she thought everything was a souvenir. I saw her pick up a nail and put it into her handbag, and when she came up to the Pennsylvania coal monument in the Mining building, she commenced putting pieces of the coal in her pocket. Then one of the working men played really a mean joke on her. He came up with a lump as big as a water bucket. Then he asked her if she wouldn't like to have that to remember the Fair by. And what do you think, she just said she thought he was very kind, but she didn't believe she could take it, for it was so big. But she would like awfully to have it. I saw the man shut one eye and say to the other man that the woman was crazy, because it was just the same kind of coal that she put into the stove every day at home."

"Now the only thing I've got to grumble about," said Uncle, "is what's models and what's facts. There is no use of scaring people to death with things that ain't so. Now over in the Government building I saw some hop plant lice that was not less than a foot long; there was a potato bug nine inches long, and there was a chinch bug two feet long, for I out with my rule and measured it. When I seen them I said, the Lord help the people who live where them things do, and then some city folks laughed at me, when at last Fanny came along and said they was models. Then we went into another room and there was soldiers from everywhere and army things that made me believe I was back again with Sherman, but there again they were wax, excepting the wagons and guns. I went up to one of the officers when I fust come in and I says, says I, "Are you regular army folks or Illinois militia?" and he didn't answer, and I turned to one of the privates and I asked why there was so many of them bunched together, then I seed some folks a laughing at me and I slunk away. I say the government is in poor business when it makes sport of its own defenders."

**"A SOUVENIR FOR HER."**

"Over there in the Transportation building I seen what it said was the boat

Columbus sailed in; but after all, Fanny said it was a model. Right close to it was the boat what Grace Darling rowed out into the storming sea and saved so many lives. I thought it was a model, but Fanny said it was the very boat she used. I jest thought ef that was really the boat, we could all be sure that Grace Darling didn't stand o' Sunday mornins afore the glass a paintin' and a powderin'." He was getting himself worked up to the belief that he was a very much abused old soldier, when Fanny said:

"Grandpa, I have just cut a splendid piece of poetry out of the paper about the Fair. The man who wrote it don't live far from us, for his address says at the bottom, 'Mr. Matthews, from Effingham County,' and I'm going to keep it in my scrap-book. Let me read it to you:

*The City of the Workers of the World*

## THE BUILDING OF IT

*In a wilderness of wonders they are piling up the stores*
*Gathered by the hands of labor on a hundred happy shores;*
*In a palpitating plexus of white palaces they heap*
*The marvels of the earth and air—the treasures of the deep;*
*They have reached their restless fingers in the pockets of the past,*
*And robbed the sleeping miser of the wealth he had amassed—*
*To the festival of nations—to the tournament of toil,*
*They have garnered in the offerings of every sun and soil;*
*They have levied on the genius of the age, and it replies*
*Full handed, with the blessed light of heaven in its eyes;*
*In honor of old Spain they have taxed the brawn and brain*
*Of a planet, for the glory of that Master of the Main,*
*Whose fortitude is written on each flag that is unfurled*
*Above the great white city of the world.*

### THE MEETING OF THE NATIONS

*They are climbing over mountains, they are sailing over seas,*
*From the artics, from the tropics, from the dim antipodes;*
*In the steamship, in the warship, under banners loved the best,*
*They are laughing up the waters from the east and from the west;*
*From the courts of Andalusia, from the castles of the Rhone,*
*To the meeting of the brotherhood of nations they are blown;*
*From the kraals beside the Congo, from the harems of the Nile,*
*They are thronging to the occident in never-ending file;*
*From the farthest crags of Asia, from the continents of snow,*
*The long-converging rivers of mankind begin to flow;*
*In the twilight of the century, its wars forever past,*
*The nations of the universe are clasping hands at last*
*By Columbia's inland waters, where in beauty lies impearled*
*The imperial white city of the workers of the world.*

### THE PASSING OF THE PAGEANT

*When the roses of the summer burn to ashes in the sun,*
*When the feast of love is finished, and the heart is overrun;*
*When the hungry soul is sated and the tongue at last denies*
*Expression to the wonders that are wearing out the eyes,*
*Then the splendor it will wane like a dream that haunts the brain,*
*Or the swift dissolving beauty of the bow above the rain;*
*And the summer domes of pleasure that bubble up the sky*
*Will tumble into legends in the twinkling of an eye;*
*But the art of man endureth, and the heart of man will glow*
*With reanimated ardor as the ages come and go.*
*The pageants of the present are but pledges of a time*
*When strifes shall be forgotten in a cycle more sublime*
*When the fancies of the future into golden wreaths are curled*
*O'er the dim, remembered city of the workers of the world.*

# CHAPTER VIII

## LA RABIDA

It was a warm summer day, and rolling chairs, launches and gondolas were in great demand. At Fanny's suggestion they decided to take an electric launch and go around to La Rabida, where the relics of Columbus were kept. She accosted one of the guards who attends to the moorings by asking how near the launch would take them to La Rabida.

"La-Ra-La what? I don't think I know what that is," said the guide.

"La Rabida is the convent—the Columbus relics are there. Columbus was the man who discovered America," Aunt volunteered to tell him.

"Oh, yes; I have heard of Columbus, of course, but I haven't been here very long."

"Well, the convent is over at the lake end of the Agricultural building. Do the launches go there?"

"The Agricultural building? Let me see; that is over——"

"Do you know where the colonnade is?"

"No. I don't."

"Ever hear of the grand basin, the gold statue, the lagoon?"

"Oh, yes; this is the lagoon."

"Well, how long will it be before a launch will come along?"

**"BEFORE THEM WAS THE STRANGE OLD CONVENT."**

He went out to the edge of the landing and looked up the lagoon. Then he jerked out, "in three-quarters of a minute." He was provoked about something. It may have been because she wanted to know so much; it may have been for a latent discovery of a lack of knowledge on his part, or it may have been because Fanny had been laughing at something; Fanny laughs easily. She is just as likely to laugh where she ought to cry; the electric guard didn't see anything to laugh at. They sat down on a pile of lumber to wait the three-quarters of a minute. It was three-quarters, and several more. The guard said the warm weather had come unexpectedly. They would have the whole fifty-two launches running soon. But only about half the number had been necessary until now, and they were very busy and could not keep up the time. One came soon after that. As they were stepping in Fanny asked how much the round trips were. Some one said "25 cents in the Director General's schedule, but in the launches they are 50 cents." The captain, or the man who takes the money, heard him. He smiled, and charged them 25 cents apiece to La Rabida. Just afterward a man handed him $1 and said "Administration building—for two." The Administration building is considerably this side of La Rabida. The captain slipped the dollar into his pocket and passed on to the next. The woman said:

"Did he keep the whole of it?"

"Keep it? I should think he did. You don't get much back on these side experiences. I ought to have asked him how much it costs to go all the way."

But the man made no reply. He was meditating. He evidently had not read the morning papers. They gave all the prices—admissions and extra convenience.

It was with feelings of considerable curiosity, mingled with awe, that they approached La Rabida.

Before them was the strange old building which they knew was the convent where Columbus had received such rest, comfort and inspiration in his great enterprise that opened the door to modern civilization.

A number of tents were on the south of the house, and soldiers were to be seen standing about, with their heavy muskets, which mean nothing but that their lives are pledged to protect this collection, belonging to the Vatican and the descendants of Columbus. All the royal letters patent from the sovereigns of Spain to Columbus and many letters written by Columbus himself, are in the cases. His will is also there. The signature of Columbus is written in this way:

*S.*
*S. A. S.*
*X. N. Y.*
*Xpo Ferens.*

At one end of this room is the collection of pictures loaned from the Vatican by Pope Leo. No one is allowed to go up the steps. One of the Columbian guards standing there said, in answer to one of Uncle's questions:

"This is the altar. It is sacred and no one is allowed up there, because these pictures are very valuable and very small."

The mention of the size in that connection meant that they could be carried off easily. But nothing could be carried off easily with those watchful "regulars" about. A contract was made by Spain with the United States before the collection left there that it should be guarded by a detachment of United States soldiers. That contract is fulfilled to the letter. No one is allowed even to touch the glasses of the case.

There are some wonderful pictures on the wall of Musaico Filato, which belong to Pope Leo. They are wonderfully beautiful as pictures, without thought of the thousands of tiny mosaics used in making the pictures, and that each one was placed in by hand. Some of the other pictures are wonderful, too—wonderful in their hideousness. No two artists seem to have the same idea of the features of Columbus. There seemed to be but one thing that they agreed upon fully, and that was that Columbus wore his hair chopped off on his neck. There is a great likeness there. Ferdinand and Isabella looked painfully disturbed on being trotted out at this World's Fair, and just exactly as if they never could have agreed on allowing Columbus or any one else to discover us. Some of the pictures were not numbered, and some of them had two numbers. The young lady who sold catalogues said they would be all right after a while.

"Say, can you tell me—is these 'ere things all Columbus' works—did 'e do 'em all?" asked Uncle.

"No, it is the history of his life."

"Didn't he do any of 'em?"

When the young lady shook her head, Uncle walked away, disappointed. He knew just what it was to dig and toll down on his farm, and he could gauge greatness only by labor. And if Columbus did not do any of it, paint any of the pictures, or build the convent, he could not understand what had made them go to so much expense to build the old convent when a good picture for a few dollars would serve just as well.

After going through the narrow entrance of La Rabida they found little dark rooms with pictures and maps and charts of Columbus and Isabel in many different forms. In the southwest room they found a table and doors and bricks and the key from the house of Columbus. In the case among the many sacred relics was a locket said to contain some of the dust of that great man. They saw the Lotto portrait which was used on the souvenir half dollars. There were the Indian idols which Columbus brought to Isabel, one of the canoes in which the Indians came out to meet him, and even one of the bolts to which Columbus was chained. Each one of the party were continually discovering the most wonderful things. Fanny found an autograph letter of the great Cortez and she wrote in her note book from the book of Waltzeemuller where he said, "Americus has discovered a fourth part more of the world and Europe and Asia are named for women this country ought to be called America or land of Americus because he has an acute intellect."

While she was writing this an old gentleman came up to her and said, "Say, Miss, I want to see the remains of Columbus, I heard they are here with a soldier on each side of his body."

Fanny pointed to the place where the locket was but he was disappointed and did not care to go "just to see a pinch of dust in a locket."

Aunt was sitting on her camp stool in the room where the table of Columbus was, but to get a nearer view of something she left it for a moment. Just then a family of man and wife with five children came in and found that they were standing at the table and by the door of Columbus. The woman saw the chair and supposing it to be a part of the Columbus furniture sat down in it. Then she arose and called her husband. "Henry come here and set in this chair. Thank God I've set where Columbus set." The husband sat in it awhile and then each one of the children time about, while Aunt Sarah waited patiently for them to get through, not wanting to break the pleasure of their great achievement.

## "THANK GOD I'VE SET WHERE COLUMBUS SET."

Tired of further sight seeing, our family decided to leave the grounds, and started on their homeward journey with over two hours ahead of them. There was no use walking through streets when they could pass nearly the whole distance through buildings. This was one of the ways to economize on travel and time.

Across the bridge from La Rabida was the great archway entrance of the Agricultural hall. Around the old convent with its low-browed walls ran a width of fresh dirt at intervals over which were stuck the ancient signs, "Keep off the grass," but no grass was yet visible.

"That's what I don't like about this White City. So much of it is so, and so much of it ain't so that I never can tell what is so," said Uncle.

In the Agricultural hall there were never ending wonders for the farmer. All the agricultural ingenuity of the earth was centered here.

"Now, come on, father, we can see plows and lawn mowers when we get home."

But Uncle lingered longingly over a new device for lacerating the soil and destroying its noxious productions. Uncle and Aunt had ceased their usual exclamations after the first two or three days. In the first place exclamations, such as the good deacon would use, were entirely inadequate, and in the second place the cords of utterance had become exhausted.

"Well, ef they haint gone and got some dog fennel here. I wonder where the cuckle-burrs are, and the tick-seed, and the jimson weeds and the puff-balls. It's a mean discrimination to bring one of the nuisances without bringing them all."

They went through and out over the bridge of the south canal, on past the bandstand to the Administration building.

"What inspiring music," said Fanny. "It is hard to tell whether our eyes or our ears can bring us the most joy. Surely I can live to be a better woman now every day of my life."

As they entered the Administration building they saw a man in the center of the court looking up through the building at the great dome which seemed to pierce the sky. He leaned farther and farther back until he fell backwards and lay there on his back still gazing intently upward. A number of people rushed up to him horror stricken, as if he had just fallen from the top of the dome and they expected to see him a crushed mass. As they began to close up around him he yelled out: "O you get away you fool people, you don't know what a fine view I'm a getting of the top."

"HIS HALF-DOLLAR ENTRANCE FEE GAVE HIM THE RIGHT TO SEE THE DOME FROM THE MOST ADVANTAGEOUS POSITION."

But one of the Columbian guards seemed to think that was not the legal way to view the dizzy heights of the building and forthwith jerked him to his feet and ushered him to the outside. The last seen of the man he was muttering, "Them fool builders put them picters clear up at the top and then the fool guards wont let a fellow enjoy them."

He evidently believed he had been treated outrageously in a free country by an autocratic guard, and that his fifty cents entrance fee entitled him to view any object in any position of vantage.

They went on into the Mines building where the sparkling ores of a thousand mines were in piles and pyramids or wrought into colonnades, facades and burnished domes. There were dazzling diamonds and beautiful opals, emeralds and gems from all parts of the earth; Michigan's copper globe, North Carolina's pavilion of mica designs, Montana's famous Rehan statue of solid silver resting on a plinth of gold, Arizona's old Spanish arastra and New Mexico's mining cabin.

From a northwest doorway they passed on out of this world of subterranean wonders across the street into the Transportation building.

"I don't believe these things are used anywhere," said Johnny. "They're like the four-legged woman—just made for show. Father, you can't expect me to ride in no common farm wagon after bringin' me to see this."

"These cars do represent awful improvement in three generations," said Uncle. "Now, it is supposed that when I was a boy I rode in that 'Flyer' there, or on the one they call 'Rocket;' but I didn't, 'cause I never seed a train till I was past twenty. Fanny would be supposed to ride up there in that gay three-story palace on wheels, and Johnny will get to ride a hundred and fifty miles an hour on that 'lectric railroad; but a common cattle car is fast enough for me. I don't know what the world's a comin' to when people rides a hundred and fifty miles an hour and choose to sleep fourteen stories high."

They had wandered around the locomotive section, and on their way curiously viewed the famous "John Bull," the oldest locomotive in America. Near by some workingmen throwing a pile of dirt into a cart, caught Uncle's eye.

"Well, look at them fellers. Ef my farm hands was to work that way I'd not get enough corn to feed my Jerseys a month."

## "A FIGHT, A FIGHT!"

He was quite disgusted with their slow and listless movements. They returned down another aisle and came out in front of the magnificent doorway of the building. They were just behind two elegantly dressed ladies, who were looking up at the decorations.

"Well, upon me wohd, do obswerve that dohway. How intwesting. I am shuah it seems to me to be pewfectly supub. It is so lovie, so sreet."

"O Grandpa," said Johnny, "do tell me what language they are talking."

"I don't know, Johnny; ask Fanny."

John's attention was here caught by the loud arguments of some gondoliers at the landing near by, and he ran down to see the fight he was sanguine enough to believe was about to take place.

They made noise enough to be sure but perhaps this was their way of attracting attention. There were at least a dozen excited foreigners gesticulating over some exciting topic. Evidently some foreigner had been riding and he thought the fare was too high. Noise and genteel swearing were the chief argument.

*They swore in German, French and Russian;*

*In Greek, Italian, Spanish, Prussian;*
*In Turkish, Swedish, Japanese—*
*You never heard such oaths as these.*
*They scolded, railed and imprecated,*
*Abased, defied and execrated;*
*With malediction, ban and curse*
*They simply went from bad to worse;*
*Carramba! O, bismillah! Sacre!*
*(And ones than which these aren't a marker.)*
*The very air with curses quivered*
*As each his favorite oath delivered;*
*A moment's pause for breath, and then*
*Each buckled up and cursed again.*

But the storm ceased as quickly as it had begun and in a minute they were all as complacent and jolly as children.

Fanny read aloud to her grandfather the words over the archway:

"There be three things which make a nation great and prosperous: a fertile soil, busy workshops, and easy conveyance for men and goods from place to place."

"Grandpa, Bacon wrote that and he lived in the time of Shakespeare, when Elizabeth was Queen of England."

"Yes, yes, child, it's a great prophesy of our greatness. I thought before I came here that the soil done about all of it and what little was not done by the soil was done by the workshop but I see that there is just as much necessity and greatness outside of these things."

"Grandpa, let me read what is on the right side of the doorway: "Of all inventions, the alphabet and the printing press alone excepted, those inventions which abridge distance have done most for civilization." That was Macaulay, the great essayist and historian of England. I wish I had known he said that, for last month we debated in our literary society the question: "Resolved. That bullets have done more for the spread of civilization than books.""

It is rather an amusing thing to note how the exposition affects different people. Some of the visitors are of a type which nothing moves. They have lived all their lives in the pursuit of a placid routine of simple duties, and, while they have come to the fair from a sense of duty and fully intend to see all that may be seen, still they are prone to retire on occasion to some quiet corner where they can rest unobserved, and then their talk invariably drops into some simple, natural channel that is in accord with the tenor of their dally lives. Of course this is tinctured more or less with the unaccustomed sights and sounds about them, but not greatly so; for the most part they simply ignore their surroundings.

In strong contrast are the ones who have obviously got themselves up expressly for the fair regardless of expense; their clothes are new, and are chiefly noticeable for the quality which Stevenson refers to as "a kind of mercantile brilliancy." They are nearly as much occupied in allowing others the inestimable pleasure of gazing at them as they are in improving their own minds. They are visitors, pure and simple, and they are characterized by such an air of newness that even the flies avoid them for fear of sticking to the varnish.

There is the girl with the notebook, a schoolmarm presumably, though heaven only knows, she may be a lecturer. She usually numbers glasses and a dark velvet bag among her accoutrements.

She is possessed of all of the catalogues and guide books sold on the grounds, and in the bag is a further supply of heavier literature for the improvement of her idle moments. It would puzzle anybody to find out when these idle moments occur, for when visible she is engaged in a frantic rush from place to place, pausing only for a moment to ask a question or jot down an impression, sometimes doing both at once without even looking at the dispenser of information.

She must have a miscellaneous mind, this girl, for anything seems to go with her from pig iron to poetry. One of her stopped for an instant in the Electricity building to inquire the name of a queer, compact, powerful looking machine. The impression which she received from the laconic attendant in charge went into her notebook in this form:

Multiple intensifier is round and black; looks powerful; attendant says 360 horse power. Mem., look up multiple intensifiers in Century dictionary on return, and find how they are applied to horses.

The machine in question was a dynamo, but perhaps she will never know.

In the Japanese section of the Manufactures building two dear little old women sat down to rest their tired feet in the midst of a bewildering display of pottery, whose brilliant tints contrasted strongly with the rusty crape and bombazine in which they were dressed.

"I don't see," said one of them, "the use of sending missionaries to Japan. I suppose they do worship all them things, but, even if they do, I think that if they had as much pretty china to home as they've got here, I'd be inclined to worship it myself. I just don't see how they can help doing it. Do you?"

"No, I don't," said the other. "It seems almost what you could expect. I don't believe they are so very bad after all. I can't believe that anyone who could make such lovely things could be a very wicked heathen. I should think the Japanese would almost feel like sending missionaries over here."

But Fanny was of a different type, she realized the sublime display of mind and she grew months in the excellence of womanhood every hour of her enthronement in the soul of this great panorama of intellect and labor. Aunt was silently seeing everything like the great dream that it was but Uncle was storing his mind with facts whereby he could confound his neighbors.

"It really seems strange to me," said Fanny, "to see how some of these people take the Fair for a circus. If the band played all the time they would never get a chance to look inside the buildings. The moment they get within earshot of the tuba horns they anchor themselves to benches or camp-stools and watch the leader swish the air with his baton. After the music stops they will begin hunting for more excitement, and may finally wander in among the pictures and admire some battle scene covering a whole wall. To-day I saw a young man and his girl standing before that wonderful statuary from the Trocadero palace looking the goddess in the eye while both were eating peanuts. They are after nothing but a good time, as at a country fair. I believe it is all because they don't understand what they are looking at. Grandpa, I can finish my education now and know how to bless you for your goodness to me. I am just beginning to see what a great privilege it is to live."

# CHAPTER IX
## THE PLAISANCE PROPHECY

Fanny had made the acquaintance of one of the ladies in charge of the educational exhibit of one of the states, and who occupied rooms on the grounds. This lady made arrangements for Fanny to remain over night with her and view a sunrise on the lake and over the "White City." It was to be an experience well in keeping with her emotional nature.

The morning came, and the two placed themselves where they could see through the columns of the peristyle across the lake in the direction of the sun. They were sitting on their camp stools on the bridge east of the statue in the basin with their cloaks drawn tightly around them, waiting in awe as they saw the suffusions of color spread upward into the grey sky.

Suddenly there is a flash of fire far out on the lake. The last pink curtain of mist rolled slowly away light and fleecy as cotton wool, and the sun, behind this lazy apparel of his rising, spreads a crimson glow over the sky and lake. Miles it comes across the rippling waves, stealing through each arch and pillared opening of the peristyle, creeping over the motionless waters of the basin and bringing brightness everywhere.

Slowly the great ball of fire rises higher. Now it flashes upon the statue of liberty, now on Diana, aiming her arrow down into the laughing waters. Under its rays the winged angels on the spires of the palace of mechanic arts seem to start into life, as if they had but paused for an instant in their flight toward the land of dawning.

Now the statues of the seasons, flanking the four corners of the Agricultural building, greet the day. Columbus, his face ever toward the west, rides onward with the sun in his triumphal car. He looks down on the work wrought out to his glory and honor, but his journey is westward still, out of the sunlight into the gloom. Against the dark western sky hangs the majestic dome of the Administration building, now a blaze of ivory and gold.

The sun lifts slowly out of the water. Its rays shine white and clear. The tired guards lean wearily over the parapets of the canals, throwing bread to hungry swans. Flocks of seabirds sweep up and down the canals like the first flurries of autumn snow. The water fowl greet the day with joyous clamor, adding a quaint, rural touch, almost startling in this city of silent palaces. They splash about the wooded island, screaming lustily when boys come in skiffs to steal their eggs. Swallows and frowsy little sparrows flit from their nests, built in the very hands of the golden goddess of Liberty.

From the roofs of every building there is a sudden flash of color. A thousand flags float in the morning breeze. Ten thousand workmen hurry through the sunny park.

The mystical city of dreamland is again the workshop of the world.

Three hours later our family were together in the art gallery glancing at the famous paintings and statues which the nations had given to show what subtle art can achieve on canvas and stone.

Aunt said she always knew those French people were the most shocking people in the world. How different their section of paintings from those of the United States. Fanny had no time for any thought outside of the overwhelming beauty of all she saw. She had begun to paint a little and to do some molding, and she knew how to appreciate the marvelous skill before her. She saw very few people who saw anything in them but a show. Uncle was positively disgusted, and went through only as if it was his duty to see everything. But among the statuary he found some things of more interest.

"Why, Grandpa, how solemn you look. Now, I can't feel solemn at this piece of statuary. Let's see what is its name. Here it is—'The Struggle for Bread.' That makes it more interesting. The people are starving and the factories can give work only to a few. Every day they throw out tickets from the windows, and whoever brings a ticket to the office window is employed. Look at that strong young man. He has secured one and the old man is pleading for it, and the woman with her little child has been knocked down in the struggle of the people for the ticket."

"Yes, yes, child, you can appreciate only the romance and sentiment of it. You have never struggled in despair for bread, and may God keep you! but Sarah and me have seen many sad, weary days of struggles to live."

Johnny had little care for the sentiment or the romance. He was much amused, but it was a dull place for him. At last a thought struck him. He struggled with it several minutes in a very deep study before he ventured to reveal his perplexity. At last it became too great to be borne longer.

"Say, Grandpa, I kin see why the sculpture can't sculpture clothes on their folks; but I don't see why the painters can't paint their folks up some more decent."

That same thing puzzled Uncle, and he could not answer. He thought a great deal, but he only muttered something about pictures not fit to be stuck on his horse-lot gate posts.

It was nearly eleven o'clock when Fanny and Aunt found Uncle and Johnny sitting disconsolately on the steps of the south entrance awaiting their appearance.

John was patriotic and he wanted to see the liberty bell over in the Pennsylvania building. A great crowd was gathering as they came up and Johnny found out that the interest came from the fact that the Duke of Varagua, the representative of Spain at the Fair and the descended of Columbus, was visiting the bell. It was a sight to awaken memory for the representative of the fifteenth century discovery to be paying respects to the representative of nineteenth century liberty.

**"NOT FIT TO STICK ON OUR HORSE-LOT GATE POST."**

City folks were not there alone. Many country people were enjoying the pulses of freedom, liberty and patriotism. An honest looking plow boy standing near Fanny asked his father what he thought of the "Dook," a real live "Dook."

"I think the dook ort to be proud of hevin' been kin to Columbus, but I'll be blamed ef I don't think Columbus would be proud too, if he wuz yer, and could tech hands 'ith his forty-eleventh grandson. It takes a purty good man to stand all the honors levished 'pon him that the dook's a-gittin' 'ithout his head a-bein' turned, an' I jes' say good fur the dook."

"It's all right to hev smart kin folks afore you, but it takes lots o' hustlin' in these days an' lots o' hard work in order to stand fust; an I vote the dook is a fine represen'tive o' his Columbus grandfather. Now lets git closer to the old lib'ty bell."

As the rural philosopher looked upon the bell hanging there in the Pennsylvania State building he said, unconscious of the crowd around him:

"When thet bell kep' a ringin' out lib'ty, the folks thet wuz they didn't know thet in a little mor'n a hundred years the hull world would be a bowin' to thet bell; an' they never hed no idee it would be carried away out yere in a place called Chicago, covered over 'ith flowers an' gyarded by perlice to keep folks from a techin' it, a fearin' harm might cume to it—an' it a standin' as a symbol o' great faith an' courage. I'm powerful glad I kin stand yere to-day with my fam'ly and look at thet bell. I jes' wisht they'd let it ring onct."

But there were others too ignorant or stupid to be patriotic before such a scene.

John became indignant, almost to the fighting point, at the amazing stupidity of some of the remarks concerning the bell. To him it was more than an emblem, it was a hero.

He heard comments which are past belief. Of course, there are patriots who approach with reverence and understanding and who are only restrained by the police from chipping off pieces of the bell, but many enter and gaze and depart in bland ignorance.

"By jinks! but that's an old feller," exclaimed one inspired ignoramus. "Wonder where it came from." Another, a stout, prosperous, business-looking party, observed that it was cracked. "Reckon that was done bringing it here," he said. "The railroads are fearful careless about handling freight."

Still another intelligent communicator, and it seemed as if nothing short of positive inspiration could justify his views, spoke of the bell slightingly as a poor exhibit, and wondered what the Pittsburg foundries meant by sending such stuff to an international exhibition.

It was now noon lunch time, and our happy family went over to a table in one of the cafes. At one o'clock Uncle and Aunt were to occupy rolling chairs in spending the afternoon sight-seeing around Midway Plaisance. They had heard a great deal about the sights there, and concluded it best to see the outside first and prepare a campaign of sight-seeing based on information received from the chair pushers.

Across the table from them sat a man eating his meal in a fatigued sort of way that caught their attention.

"Good evening, Colonel," said a gentleman, coming up to him. The colonel was not himself, that was plain. His eyes looked dreamy, and he had the appearance of a man who was under the influence of some strong and very pleasurable excitement. When the friend saluted him he did not reply with marked courtesy. He did not even look at him. He continued to gaze unmeaningly at his plate, and to murmur "Irene-te-raddle, fol de-rol. I'll niver go there anny more."

"What's the matter with you?" asked the gentleman, testily.

"Well, sir, it do beat the dickens," said the colonel, irreverently, "I've lived a long toime an' seen manny a queer soight in circuses an' dime musooms an' hanky-panky shows, but niver till to-day—oh! Naha-a, it's a bright eyes an'—a bonny locks—" here the colonel began to thrum the table.

The friend came over impatiently and shook his fist under the colonel's nose.

"You weak-minded old gazabo, is it to hear ye singin' topical songs thot Oi came down from Archery road? What ails ye?"

The colonel remarked easily: "Don't git gay, George; don't git gay. Because Oi chuse to sing a little is no reason why ye should take liberties." Then he went on, half-musing: "Oi don't give annything for the Fair itsilf. O'Connor tuk me in there first, but what do Oi ca-are for show cases full uv dhried prunes, ould r-rocks an' silk handkerchers? I was f'r goin' over to see Buffalo Willie shootin' Injuns an' rescuin' Annie Oakley frum the red divvels, but O'Connor sez: 'No,' he sez, 'come on an' see the Midway,' he sez. 'So over we goes to the Midway, an', George, Oi haven't been well since. There'll be a trolley in me hed to me dhyin' dhay, there will, there will. We had no more than got in the strate when a nigger in a mother Hubbard comes up an' sez: 'Little mon.'

"'Yis,' sez I, 'an' dom ye little mon till ye do go home an' put on ye're pants, ye bould thing.'

"'Hugh-h!' sez O'Connor; 'that's a Turk.'

"'Thin there's a pair of us,' I sez; 'let's go.'

"'Well,' he sez, 'come into the Turkish village.'

"'An' see more niggers? I'll not,' I sez.

"'Will you go to the Irish village, thin?'

"'No,' I sez, 'aint I seen you?'

"'Well, where will you go?'

"'If you know a place where they keep beer,' I sez, 'I'm convenient.'

**"DOM YE, LITTLE MON," SAYS I, "TILL YE DO GO HOME AN'
PUT ON YER PANTS."**

"He shoots me into a hole in the ground. George, ye should a seen it! At one table sat a lot of black fellows with red towels around their heads an' knives stickin' out of their yellow cloaks. At another table was half-a-dozen gurrls with earrings as big as barrelhoops in their ears.

"'Come on back,' sez O'Connor.

"'No,' I sez, 'this is good enough for a poor man,' an' we sat down at the next table to th' gurrls. Well, sir, from that time my mind's a blank. I was like the feller in the story-books. I knew no more. I dunno what happened at all, at all, with dancin' gurrls an' snake cha-armers an' Boolgarian club swingers an' foreign men goin' around with their legs in mattesses. All I know is this, that I was carried to a ca-ar in a seedin' chair by two men with room enough in the seat of their pants to dhrive a street sweeper. Did y'r never ride in a seedin' chair, George? Then, faith, ye're not in my class. Fol-der-rol, de-rol de raddle, fol——"

"An' what did ye do with O'Connor?"

"How do I know? The last time I remimber him he was askin' a girl in the Turkish theayter whether she liked vanilla or rawsburry in her soda wather, the droolin jackanapes. Ah, na-ha, the girls of Limerick city——." The colonel resumed his thrumming.

"And is that all you see of the fair."

"Yis," said the colonel, "an" faith! if you had me hed you'd think it was enough. An', George, to be in earnest wid ye, that I've known since you was a little dirty boy, go to the fair, ride around in the boats, luk at the canned tomatties an' the table-clothes, ride in the electric cars, but beware of that Midway. It'll no do for young men at all, at all. You'd lose your head. You would, you would. Oh, fol-de-rol, de raddle rol."

After this amusing experience just related before them, Uncle thought it very advisable to give Johnny "a good talkin' to about doin' nothin' wrong in that heathen exhibition of furriners."

But Johnny could afford to finish that Saturday walking demurely around with the rest, for the next Monday morning Louis, the train-boy, was to be guard and guide through the mysteries of Midway Plaisance.

# CHAPTER X

## PLAISANCE SOCIETY

When Monday morning came the family were promptly at the 60th street gate at nine o'clock. Johnny espied Louis with his eye over a knot hole that seemed designed by providence to let the hungry outsiders have a morsel of the Midway Plaisance scenery. Inside of the grounds Johnny determinedly led the way at once to the great Ferris go-round. They stood before it measuring their chances of living through such a revolution. It did not take much to persuade Fanny to accompany the venturesome boys; Uncle positively refused to discuss such a piece of folly, but Aunt decided at last that if Fanny went she must go also.

Like a forbidden specter the skeleton of the Ferris Wheel stands out gaunt and fleshless. All around is full of light and gayety.

A devout Moslem may be pardoned if, as he passes, he touches his forehead with three fingers of his right hand and murmurs: "Allah il Allah!" Some such exorcism seems to be needed to ward off the evil spirits that one would think must cluster around the ponderous structure, perching, perhaps, like the broomstick riders of Salem, on its spare metal ribs.

They entered the car of the great wheel, and when the signal to start was given they found that another old lady with her dudish son were to be their companions in the aerial flight.

The earth was dropping away. Higher and higher they went. Johnny was holding with a death-like grip on to the car. Fanny's whole life was passing before her like a procession of spectres. In a few minutes they had gone more than one hundred and fifty feet, and the sky seemed to be falling upon them.

"Stop her!" shouted the dude, accompanying his words with a frantic waving of his hands. Higher yet they ascended and his face assumed the look depicted in the features of Dante's characters when about to enter the infernal regions.

## "HIS PLANS IN LIFE WERE INTERFERED WITH."

"Now, if the good Lord ever permits me to get back to the earth safely," said the old woman, "I promise never to leave it again till I am called to die."

They had reached the top and passed the crisis of going up. Now they began to fall. The sky was leaving them, and the earth was coming after them. They had no time to think. The coming down was worse than the going up. When they stepped out on the earth at the bottom of their descent it was with a sensation of thankfulness never experienced before.

The wheel is 275 feet high, and requires over 500 horse power to turn it. The axle is the largest piece of steel ever forged, and it was a great triumph of engineering skill to put it in place 150 feet from the ground.

Hagenbeck's animal show was naturally the next attraction. Some distance ahead of them there was quite a commotion. Johnny and his companion were, as usual, ahead. In another minute Johnny came running back to Fanny and caught her by the hand. Without a word he started forward with her at a rapid pace. Quite a crowd was following some strange object, and Johnny hurried Fanny around to the front, where she saw Mr. Hagenbeck coming leisurely toward them with a lion walking by his side. This was the object which was attracting such a large crowd of people, and it indeed took some courage to stand there as he came by. So completely did they all acknowledge the superiority of the animal that there was no jostling about him. The Columbian guards did not have to form a line—in fact, even they gave way to the distinguished walker who held his head high in the air and enjoyed the bright sunshine without deigning to look at the crowd of different races around him. He was a native of India, and was born to be a king, but his plans in life were interfered with, and the forest in which he was to have ruled was invaded and he was captured. For some time he had not been feeling well, and the proprietor determined to let the captive see the sunshine. So they started out together, the lion walking along as quietly as a spaniel. When the six lions in the cage saw their comrade out for a stroll they gave a chorus of roars which made the windows rattle. It was answered from the roadway, and six guards who stood by thought discretion the better part of valor, and started on a run for the viaduct. Mr. Hagenbeck called them back and told them it was all right, but they still kept a safe distance. The lion seemed to enjoy the outing, yet when his trainer started to come back the monarch of the jungle followed him.

The crowd parted as the pair came toward it with more haste than grace, and the lion licked his companion's hand and went back to his cage. Mr. Hagenbeck explained that the lion is one of the largest in the world, and is not yet full grown. It is perfectly gentle, and at his home in Hamburg it is not kept in a cage, but plays in the yard with his children like a cat.

In front of Hagenbeck's building there were assembled a motley crowd of people gazing into a small room over the entrance way. There were a number of lions jumping about at the crack of the master's whip and giving the people a sample show of what could be seen inside. It caught the crowd, for there was a rush to the ticket office when the keeper disappeared from among the lions.

In the center of the building was a circular cage that looked like an old fashioned wire rat trap greatly enlarged. Into this cage the animals were introduced to go through with their performance.

"Well for that bear to walk on that globe and roll it along beats anything I ever seed," said Uncle. "He's got more agility in him than I ever had even at my best. Johnny, you couldn't walk a log across the creek as well as that bear walks that pole, and just look at him walking backwards. If you will notice, Johnny, you will see that the trainer gives all that acts bad a lump of sugar and the ones that act good don't get nothing. That's the way of lots of things, but if you will notice it the good ones will live the longest."

Aunt admired the dogs very much and observed that they didn't have to be told what to do as the others did and they were more willing and more grateful for attention. It was really pathetic and comical to see how they seemed to appreciate applause.

The dwarf elephant, thirty-five inches high, was brought into the arena in an ordinary trunk. It complacently ate some sugar and returned to its quarters.

When the show was over they walked up the street toward the Turkish village.

Here a number of people were gathering around a Turkish fakir who was at the side of the street loudly proclaiming the merits of his wares and shouting out some tirade that his employer had taught him as a means of attracting a crowd. Johnny had seen the fellow before and he drew his friends up close to him so they could hear his peculiar harangue.

"By the beard of the prophet, my heart swells to spill the souls of those christian dogs. I am the mighty man of the desert and they shall repent or die."

"He, he, he," yelled Louis, "that's the feller what the kids told me yanked the mummy of Rameses from the holy temple and knocks out all the Chinamen and Arabs along the Plaisance. Look at him howl."

"Oh, Jeremiah, let's get away quick. I'm 'fraid he's dangerous," said Aunt Sarah.

"No he ain't," said Louis. "Jest watch me," and he walked up and tossed a copper at the orator's head and Abdul, the mighty man of the desert, caught it with a grin and in broken English said "tank ye."

"Disturb me not, O reckless heathens," and he flipped a pebble with his fingers at a passing German who had just come out of the mediaeval castle with a tray of beer mugs on his head. The stone struck him on the ear. He set his tray down on a table and came over to the warlike Arab.

"Wot ver you trow dot stein."

"Move on I contend only with the strong and mighty."

"Wot ver you trow dot stein," and the little waiter edged up close.

**"IT STRUCK HIM ON THE EAR.**

"O mamma, I know the poor waiter will be killed, let's run away quick," said Fanny.

"O yer don't know nothin'," said Johnny, disgusted. "The Dutchman kin lick him in a minnit."

## "SHE SKETCHED THEIR HEADS ——"

"Wut ver you trow dot stein. You tink I am a house side. Donnervetter! I gif you some brains alretty;" and before Abdul, son of Cairo, could think, the little

German tripped him to the ground, and as he fell caught him by the hair and dragged him into the boundary lines of the Turkish village, slammed him on the ground, and in a few minutes was back among the beer tables of the castle with his tray, calling "peer, peer, shents! ah trei peer, two cigar, kevarter tollar!"

The day had been a very fatiguing one, and Uncle and Aunt decided to spend the next day quietly at home in the hotel. Johnny and Louis had stayed manfully by the old folks all day, and their promised adventures had not yet occurred. The next day they were to be the guardians of Fanny, and they were quite proud of the duty.

Fanny's note book and sketch book were now pretty well filled. Midway Plaisance heads and feet offered the most tempting work for her pencil. It is tempting enough for anyone to ask: "Where did you get that hat?" or "Where did you hit that shoe?" Evidently not in Chicago. Nothing of their kind ever graced a western city in such versatile varieties until the bands began to play and the world's cake-walk moved down the Plaisance.

In former years, when they had band concerts and Sunday school picnics at Jackson Park the visitor saw about four kinds of masculine headwear. One was the gray helmet of the park policeman resting under the tree. Another was the tall and shining silk hat of the elderly parent. In addition to these were some straw hats with rims not so wide as those of 1893, and derbys which were a trifle higher in the crown than the new ones. In the general description at the park the old styles of headwear have been crowded to the background by foreign novelties. The dicer, the fez, the turban, the hood, the helmet and the sun-shade are becoming very common. Only the stranger who comes into the gates is startled by the sight of a gaunt black man wrapped in a sheet and wearing coiled around his head enough clothing to make a good wash. But of all the incomprehensible varieties of headwear about the grounds from foreign lands, it remained for our own American Indian to outdo them all. When the great No Neck, of the Sioux nation, walks through the grounds with his war bonnet of eagle feathers trailing on the ground, the East Indians concede their defeat. No Neck's bonnet is worth about $400.

The footwear is worse in variety, if such a thing is possible. Perhaps, after all, it is a matter of education rather than appearance or convenience. The most elaborate is the high-topped boots of the German cavalryman, and the least the Dahomey Amazon, who sometimes has a red string tied around her great toe. They come from a torrid country, and have been freezing nearly every day, but scorn the apparel of the weak white man. The Amazons refuse to wear shoes. When it is too chilly for them to gallop around inside the bark fence they crawl into their tents, roll themselves up in the black blankets and criticise the policy of the Exposition.

On a moist day, when a Chinaman walks down the Plaisance he leaves a trail of oval-shaped tracks. It would take a keen judge of human nature to decide by looking at the tracks whether he has left home or was going back.

**"——AND THEN THEIR FEET."**

The Soudanese slipper is the most shiftless thing that a man ever put on his foot. It is simply a leather sole and toe. These represent the triumph of laziness. The Soudan citizen simply walks into his slipper in the morning and then in the evening he backs out. Every time he takes a step he lifts his heel away from the sole and it seems morally certain that he will lose the slipper, but in some way he manages to hold it. It is said this trick is accomplished by elevating the big toe at each step, thus preventing any slip. Any uncultured American who started for a promenade, wearing such things, would be in his stocking feet before he proceeded ten steps, but the men in the Cairo street tramp around all day and apparently do not realize that they are running any risk.

That evening at home Fanny gave a review of her note book, wherein she had recorded her observations on the politeness of the different nations as she had witnessed them. She thought the Javanese were the politest people of all. They always lay their hands upon their hearts and say, "I am honored," when spoken to. When they failed in their ability to answer a question, they just smile to show their good will. The Fort Rupert Indians politely tell their visitor to go when they have told what is asked for. There is of course more kinds of etiquette in the Plaisance than in any other spot of its size on earth. If the visitor desired to be just right it would require an etiquette reference book in at least sixteen languages.

Among the Turks there are strange habits. In greeting a stranger they bow very low and remain perfectly silent until spoken to. They will then shake hands in a genuine English fashion. One Turk calling on another will never sit down until the host arrives, even if he has to wait an hour. When the host comes in the two sit down after having exchanged greetings and not another word is spoken until coffee is served. The Syrians, on the other hand, will not turn their faces to a host before being spoken to. It is the proper thing when visiting one of them to take a seat with the back to the door and wait until the host enters and make no move until spoken to, when the visitor is expected to rise and bow.

To fully understand all an Egyptian says and does is a harder task than deciphering the hieroglyphics on an obelisk. The language of the Egyptian gentleman is the most fulsome possible. If he should be in need of a little temporary loan he will pound the man (whom he hopes to confidence successfully) on the back until he can hardly breathe. Experts in Egyptian etiquette can tell by the pounding process what is coming, and when the ceremony reaches the piledriver degree it is the proper thing to say: "What can I do for you?"

On hearing this the Egyptian will talk something like this: "Do for me? Why, my dear and most honored sir, your humble dog of a servant would not presume to ask a favor of one so great as you. I thought of calling on you yesterday, but it rained, and I feared that you would not be in a good humor and might refuse me, but then I want nothing. Who am I that a humble follower of Mohammed should dare to ask of you, my great lord and master, the very slightest favor? And yet if it had not rained yesterday I should have been fully inclined to ask you for temporary aid, but to-day I would not think of causing your highness any trouble. Why should I, who am so lowly, ask one for $5 for a few days. It would be an insult to you; one you could never forget. What, you insist on it? I am to take this, am I? Now really, as I was saying that one so low—but if you positively insist, if you are sure you will be deeply and terribly insulted if I do not take it—but your dog of a servant——"

That settles it. Having obtained the money he marches out without a thank you or goodbye.

The Dahomey people are the strangest of all. The first greeting of one amazon to the other is to slap her face. The visitor always slaps the hostess first, and if the visit is welcome the visitor gets a cuff on each cheek, and if it is not convenient to receive the visitor no slap is given in return.

But the palm is left to the American for a whole-souled disregard of the feelings of others. The show was brought here for the special benefit of the visitor; he has paid his money, and he has the right to do as he pleases.

If the sedan chair bearers happen to pass with some fat man for a passenger, the whole street is in an uproar of English comment meant to be humorous. Then the ordinary American visitor seems to think it his prerogative to point at the foreign contingent and say things aloud about them that would secure physical retaliation if the object of the remark were a citizen of the United States instead of a guest of the nation.

# CHAPTER XI

## A STARTLING MYSTERY

The next day was what the boys called African day; that is, they intended to see all that was to be seen from Dahomey to Nubia and Soudan. Fanny was to spend the morning in the panoramas of the Burnese Alps and the volcano Kilaueau. At noon she would meet them at one of the inns.

The boys wandered about for some time in search of adventure. Over in the street of Cairo there were two peculiar structures that looked like inverted soup-bowls. There was a three cornered aperture In the front of each where men and women could be seen crawling in and out. Over one of these doors was a placard on which was painted, "See the 18 months old Soudanese baby dance. The only dance of the kind on earth." Over the door of the other one was a placard on which was printed "Only 25c to see the great Nubian terpsichorean evolutions." Two or three men would come up, stand awhile and listen at the curious sounds from within, resembling very much the noise made by a pack of curs after a rabbit they did not hope to catch; or, perhaps, more like a plantation jamboree when all the strings of the banjo were broken but one and it had been mended twice.

The people came to see the sights, and here was a mysterious something they might regret a lifetime in the missing. Our two boys required no mental balancing of any nice points of propriety. It was there to see, and they had the money to see it with. What more was wanting? Nothing but to exchange the fee for the yellow ticket and present it to the saffron-hued keeper of the door. The little half space alloted to visitors inside was crowded, but the two boys were soon at the front. This was the Nubian's place. There were two men, two women and two little girls. All had what seemed very much like bed-sheets wrapped closely around them. The older girl, according to Johnny's estimate, was six inches through and about five feet tall. One of the men had a belt made of goat hoofs. He danced around awhile and then held out his hat for voluntary contributions. A number of nickels and dimes went in, and then a vigorous dancing commenced. The dance consisted in all jumping straight up and down as stiff-legged and as high as possible. The hat went round again, and the pennies and nickels came in by handfuls. This made them wild in their desire to give value received, and they jumped higher and higher, faster and faster. Sometimes they forgot that they were in Chicago and neglected to attend to the sheet with dexterity. But when people are in Nubia they are supposed to do as the Nubians do and not regard these little negligences. Some of the women went out, but Johnny and Louis stayed in; and they kept staying like a small boy at a free phonograph. They were studying Nubians.

After being satiated with knowledge, they remembered that there was a Soudanese baby dance, the only one of its kind on earth. They might be missing something. Then they wanted out.

In the next place they saw the same kind of people and the same dance. True, there was a baby eating some candy in the back of the hut, but its jaws did all the dancing for it. This was a swindle which the boys would not further encourage by their presence, and they withdrew.

From this they went over to the Dahomey village. Like all Gaul, Dahomey is divided into three parts, whereof Monsieur and his staff inhabit one, his warriors a second, and his amazons a third. The amazons are twenty in number and for the most part are occupied in the pursuit of keeping their pickaninnies from making mud pies with the drinking water. They live in a row of long, low huts thatched with palm leaves.

**"THE TINT OF A NEWLY BLACKED PAIR OF OXFORDS."**

A rail runs in front of the huts and a board sidewalk, on which the amazons squat to perform their toilets, mainly consisting of the application of greasy combs to the half inch of wool accorded them by their Creator to serve the purpose of hair.

Day and night they oil themselves. Other times they oil one another. Their shining bodies reflect the glory of the noonday sun. Their complexions when their toilets are fully complete approach patent leather. Other times they stop short at the tint of a newly blacked pair of Oxfords.

Inside the huts the amazons betake themselves to arts of peace. A tall woman, clad in a striped loin cloth, was rubbing corn between two big stones in a firm faith that eventually it would become meal. The miller is the curiosity of the realm, for she only has two husbands, both of whom, however, she saw fit to leave behind her in Africa to mind the babies. In Dahomey the hand that rocks the cradle does not bother about ruling the world. Woman has her rights with a vengeance among those people and man has fully recognized her fighting qualities.

They found the village tightly enclosed in a high board fence. Then began a vigorous search for knot-holes. But every opening they found had the walls of a hut before it. At last they were partially rewarded by discovering a fault in one of the boards where they could see past one of the huts into the enclosure. Half a dozen of the backs of men and women could be seen about ten steps from the fence. The people would bend over out of sight and then back again. All kinds of conjectures came to the boys. Louis suggested that they were "shootin' craps." Johnny thought they were doing some kind of a religious ceremony. The pressure of curiosity became too great to be endured. They went around the corner and discovered that there was not a single guard in sight. Johnny was standing the expenses, and Louis was generous enough to propose that some means be secured to elevate Johnny to the top of the fence. No more intense brain work was expended on the Ferris wheel than these two boys gave to the proposed elevation. It took mechanical skill of the highest order, for the management had provided for these emergencies, and there was nothing in sight to help them. But necessity kindly became again the mother of invention. There was a small tool chest a short distance down the back fence waiting for the wagon to take it away. It evidently contained no tools, for it was quite light, and the boys soon had it set on end against the fence. Louis got on top of this and was able by tip-toeing to get an occasional glimpse over. But not long enough to reach any conclusions as to the mysterious ceremonies transpiring within. Louis caught hold of the top of the fence firmly and told Johnny to climb up over his back. The natives were too intent at their work to see him, and he got astride of the fence without any difficulty, but in such a position that he could not see what was going on. The eaves of the conical shaped hut were almost in reach. He moved back a little and put his hand on the roof to steady himself. But, alas, the roof was dried palm leaves, and instead of supporting him his hand plunged through and before he could recover himself he fell crashing over against the house, held there for a moment as in despair and then with an armful of the hut held tight to his breast he fell headlong to the ground. The excited natives in all styles of dress, from the voluptuous mother hubbard, much abbreviated above and below to the heavy slouch hat and military overcoat, all crowded around him in the belief that somehow he was intending to destroy their domestic happiness.

Johnny did not know in what form the attack was coming and as he could not turn over to get up without touching one of the natives he concluded it wisest to lie still on his back with the portion of the hut which he had brought down with him, remaining over him for protection. Louis gave a mighty jump upward and got his elbows over the top of the fence. He drew himself up enough to see Johnny lying on his back so still and the natives gathered around him gesticulating wildly and talking in a very excited manner. The sight was enough. Certainly, his friend was dead. He gave a yell that could be heard to the beauty show, and jumped down to the ground, calling for the police at the top of his voice. The natives hearing the noise, supposed there was a plot to murder them all, and one got a long-handled rake some workman had left and began to pull the grass off of the prostrate Johnny. Meantime, the frantic explanations of Louis that the Dahomeys were murdering his friend brought a greater and greater crowd to the corner of the enclosure. A number of guards came up, but they had no key and no authority to break into the village. Some policemen came up, but they were either powerless or could not comprehend. No one had seen the accident, and Louis was fast becoming incoherent in his oft repeated explanations. Meanwhile the crowd grew larger and larger, till hundreds were gathered together. All the Plaisance was coming to see what extraordinary affair was taking place.

**"HE GAVE A YELL THAT COULD BE HEARD TO THE BEAUTY SHOW."**

When all the debris was pulled off of Johnny he concluded to get up. He tried to make them understand that he wanted out, but they could not get his meaning, for he was so bewildered that he was pointing in another direction from the gate. At last one seemed to comprehend, and he ran as fast as he could go to one of the huts toward which Johnny seemed to point, and returned leading one of the damsels of the place who, from gorgeousness of native modesty, seemed to be the belle of the village. The native evidently thought that Johnny was in love with the girl, and that he had taken this unceremonious method as the last desperate chance of his life to obtain her. The native was presenting her to him with all his natural suaveness, and was apparently offering him the freedom of the town, when the gate opened and two officers rushed in. One of them took Johnny by the ear and led him outside. People were packed about the place in enormous masses, and every available fence or elevation was utilized by the crowd struggling to see. A dozen or more policemen were outside endeavoring to handle the mass of people. It took half an hour for them to make a way to get John to the outside. When they saw Johnny, a great shout was set up, but it only added to the fright that already possessed Johnny's whole mind.

All sorts of stories were afloat among the people. Some said the Dahomeys had captured a boy the night before and were just on the eve of sacrificing him to their idols when a policeman got track of what was going on. As some policemen passed this part of the crowd they were cheered, cheer on cheer, for their keenness and bravery in rescuing an American from such a fate. Others, who claimed to know, said it was worse even than that, for one of the policemen had confided to him that the Dahomey people were about to practice cannibalism and had secured the boy in order to eat him. A number were sure that this would cause our government to have these people sent back to Dahomey and as they were under the French government and were brought here by French people it would probably lead to an open rupture between the two republics and perhaps involve all Europe in a struggle for national existence.

The reporters ran the rumors down to the very last prophecy and sent posthaste their scoops to their respective papers and a wave of indignation swept the entire country that cannibalism came so near being enacted in the very midst of the greatest enterprise of modern civilization.

The name of the boy could not be learned, nor anybody found who knew anything about him, but there were thousands of people who were witnesses of the rescue and bore testimony of how near our nation came of being disgraced forever. The policemen knew nothing about it. All they could say was that they found the boy surrounded by the natives, and they since remembered that he seemed too terrified to speak, and the natives were greatly excited at the presence of the officers. They had taken the boy to the outside of the crowd and let him go. The natives themselves could give only a confused account of how they had heard a noise and had seen the boy lying near one of the huts on his back and covered with material torn from the roof of one of the huts. Their story was evidently absurd. Meantime the delivery wagon had taken the tool chest away and thus destroyed the only evidence that might have cleared up the case. The fence was too high for the boy to climb over, and the Columbian guards detailed to that section swore they always kept the whole village in view, and it was impossible for the boy to have got over the fence without being seen by them. Like the great wave of the sea that breaks into a million pieces as it strikes the shore, so this great question resolved itself into a thousand theories, and at last lived in the memory of the people only as the great mystery of Midway Plaisance.

# CHAPTER XII

## BEAUTY SHOW

Fanny was at the inn when noon came but the boys were nowhere to be seen. She saw great crowds of people massed a little way up the street but crowds were a common sight. She heard broken narrations of some exciting event that had transpired but there was nothing to cause her to think that her brother might be the central figure of all the excitement. Johnny rarely missed his appointments with her and she felt that something unusual had occurred or he would have met her at the designated place.

She decided to spend the afternoon at the Libby Glass Works and at the Beauty show. Once in the works, where glass is wrought into the most curious and costly designs, a few hours seems only too short for a good appreciation of the work done. The art, as illustrated there, is as fascinating as a romance. Three hundred people are employed there daily in showing what can be done with glass. Entrance is to be had to the blowing-room, in the center of which is the huge cruciform. In this there are placed the crucibles, as the working-holes are called. The heat in the furnace is 2,000 degrees Fahrenheit.

The batch from which glass is made is composed of sand, lead, saltpetre, potash and soda. It has to be cooked in the terrible heat for twenty-four hours before it is fit for use. In front of the working holes are the workmen. A long steel tube is thrust into the batch and a quantity of the mixture accumulated on the end. From the moment it is taken out of the crucible until the form is completed the operator never allows the hot glass to be still for a moment. It is always moving.

The second floor of the building is a lively place. It is here that the cutting is done. The process is most interesting and shows the highest skill of the glass-worker's art.

Opposite the cutting department is the glass spinning and weaving department. The spinning of glass into fine threads is done by means of a wheel nine feet in diameter which revolves twenty times a minute. A glass rod is exposed at one end to a blowpipe flame. When the glass is melted it is attached to the periphery of the wheel and the operator sits with watch in front of him. Every minute the position of the melting glass is shifted until the broad wheel is filled, when it is stopped and the glass is cut and taken off, made into the desired lengths and taken to the loom. The weaving is done by girls on hand looms. Two hundred threads of glass are woven alternately with one thread of silk. The thread is made up into napkins, neckties, lamp shades, bonnets and hats.

**"SHE THOUGHT VERY DIFFERENTLY OF HIM NOW."**

Fanny sat down on a bench to rest for a while when, chancing to glance to the far side of the exhibit she saw Mr. Warner, whom she had formerly known as Mr. Moses, intently watching the work in the looms. She thought very differently of him now. Louis had hotly defended him against everything the confidence man had said, and, of course, she now saw that the man who had spoken against Mr. Warner was of the most abandoned type of men. Somehow she felt that she owed him some palliation for the rudeness she had exercised. It would, perhaps, not be altogether according to the rules of etiquette; but if the opportunity offered she intended to say something in explanation. As he came on around her way she felt her pulses beat faster and her face flushing under some strange excitement. As he approached to where she sat, he saw her and stopped for a moment. When he came by she looked, up and he bowed and was about to pass on, but she arose from her seat unde he stopped. He held in his hand some samples of woven goods, and he remarked that he was making a study of these fabrics to see if they were worth handling by his firm. The conversation led on so easily and naturally that she forgot that she had something she wanted to say in extenuation of past rudeness. She could not help observing how totally different was this man's bearing and conversation from the evil-minded man who had presumed upon her acquaintance before. There were no questions asked; no lead in conversation that caused her to speak in any way whatever of herself or her people. In a few minutes he had passed on, and she felt from instinct and reason that this man was a gentleman.

**"THE LADIES WANTED TO SEE HER DRESS."**

From this place she went over to the international dress exhibit, more commonly known as the "Beauty Show." Here were fifty young ladies chosen from as many different nationalities in order to exhibit the fashions of the world in the highest art of dress. At the front was Fatima, the queen of beauty. Her booth represented a room in the Sultan's harem. On either side, reclining on an ottoman, were her waiting maids, and at her feet her special servant. All the magnificence of oriental splendor surrounded her. A group of at least a hundred people were continually crowding the railing in front. They plied her with questions, and the ladies were much offended because she would not walk around so they could get a better view of her dress. She could answer questions in nearly any language but Turkish, and she finally admitted to some French gentlemen who were quizzing her that she came from Austria, her foot servant from the south of France, and her waiting maids from Paris.

That international beauty show is a wonderful and fearful affair. The beautiful representative of Ireland is dressed in green, and wears glasses.

"Arrah," said an Irishman to the proprietor, "raley now, is it in grane all the Oirish girruls do be drissed? By the bones av St. Patrig, 'tis the first toime Oi iver saw wan in glasses."

"The fact of the matter is that our Irish young lady is ill, and we have engaged this young lady to fill her place," said the proprietor, and he moved away only to hear the following conversation with the typical Greek lady from the Ionian isles:

"Do you speak English?" from a visitor. The lady shook her head.

"Do you speak French?" This In French by the same. Another shake of the classic head.

"Do you speak Greek?" This actually in Greek, but it only brought another shake.

"Sprechen sie Deitsch?" cried the visitor, with some impatience.

"Oh, ja! ja!" exclaimed the Greek young lady, eagerly, and a general laugh went around the little group which had listened to the conversation.

"Say, Bess," said a young fellow, nudging his girl and pointing to the Queen of Beauty, "ain't she a corker?"

"Naw," replied Bess. "I don't see anything pretty about her. She's all drug store. Anybody can see that."

"How d'ye like that, Mariar?" remarked an old Hoosier, stroking his yellow whiskers and squinting at his better half, a hawk-faced woman of determined countenance. "I tell yer what. Mariar, with all your good qualities yer never could hold a candle to that 'ere girl, could yer, now? Honest?"

"Benjamin! Come right along out o' here. Yer head's bein' turned by these brazen-faced females. Why, yer'll be cavorting around here like a young colt in a minnit or two. The idee o' comparin' me with that painted young woman—me, your loving wife—come along now," and Benjamin went.

**"THERE WAS A PERT YOUNG MISS WALKING THE FLOOR."**

At the United States booth there was a pert Miss walking the floor, monarch of all she surveyed, a typical Uncle Sam's daughter. It was a sorry mistake when a dude presumed too much on her patience or a smart young man made too free with his remarks. She was always ready for them, to the delight of the patriotic young Americans about.

Here Fanny found five young girls studying the United States beauty with more than ordinary interest. Each of the girls wore a badge, on which was printed C. C. of C. C., and just above these letters were five more, M. K. S. L. N. A note book containing a pencil was attached by a neat little chain with the badge. There was scarcely a minute that one or the other of them was not writing something in her book.

Dressed exactly alike and being so intent on their work, they were evidently not ordinary sight-seers. Finally some remark was made between Fanny and one of the girls and Fanny showed her own note and sketch book and asked how they were keeping theirs. It soon appeared that these five girls were in a contest of more than ordinary interest. An enterprising newspaper of a Southern Illinois town had sent these five girls to see the Fair. They were to be supplied with all needful money, to be independent of all escorts, to take notes and write up their adventures and their version of the scenes of the great exposition entirely unknown to one another, and the paper would publish their reports on their return. Competent judges were to decide on the merits of their work and a handsome reward would be given to the successful writer. In an adjoining town another editor had sent out five boys on the same errand. The writers must all be between twelve and fifteen. The one out of the ten who did the best work was to receive a splendid souvenir medal. They were given ten days of sight-seeing and their whole souls were in the work.

"But what can be the meaning of these letters C. C. of C. C."

"At home they say these letters mean Crazy Cranks of Cumberland County but the fact is they have a meaning which is a secret that shall die with us. We are sworn with each other never to reveal it and to prove that girls can keep secrets. Of course the letters form our club name, and it has the word Columbian in it, but that is all we are ever to tell. We have a constitution and by-laws and regular meetings for mutual protection and advice in our trials and troubles." This was all quite interesting as a proof of what the girls in the latter part of the 19th century could do. Fanny and these girls at once became fast friends, for she found that they did not live a score of miles from her home, and that there were a number of people and home places that they all knew.

"But what can these letters "M. K. S. L. N." here at the top of the badge mean?"

"Oh, that is no secret. They are the initials of our names—Mary, Kate, Stella, Leila and Nannie."

They said they were not the only ones on a like errand, for they had met a little girl all the way from Boston, and only fourteen years old, who had been sent on the same errand by her class in the high school, and they had heard of girls from the south and west who were coming for the same purpose.

"We can't lecture," said Mary, "but we are going to help the Women's Congress prove that girls have just as much brains and courage as boys."

It was now nearly six o'clock, and Fanny was so interested in the five girls that she persuaded them to go home with her to enjoy the evening together. It promised a pleasant diversion, for the five girls had been hard at work several days and had not met a single acquaintance or congenial friend.

When Fanny arrived at her hotel that evening with the five girls, it was to discover Uncle and Aunt in consternation over an extraordinary story told by Johnny, who had arrived home an hour or two before. According to his story, he and Louis had tried to see into the Dahomey village. He did not know that it was wrong. He missed his balance and fell over the fence. He was scared and stunned by his fall. After a while he heard Louis yelling as if in great pain. Then two policemen came in and protected Johnny till he got safely away. When they reached the outside of the crowd which was all the time yelling at them, the policeman told him to git if he didn't want to get mobbed. He ran as hard as he could run in order to escape. Then he remembered Louis was caught, for he had heard him calling for help. Johnny came back around the buildings, but, alas! the bloodthirsty mob had done its work and Louis was no more. Johnny, now safely at home, lay moaning on his bed and would not be comforted. Fanny remembered having seen the great crowd over by the Dahomey village, but she had not dreamed of such a terrible scene taking place. Altogether it seemed incredible.

"Extry papurs, all about de cannibal feast!"

A thought suddenly struck Fanny that if there had been such a horrible tragedy as Johnny had told of, the papers would tell all about it. She ran down to the street and came back with a copy. She looked rapidly over the paper, but she saw nothing about a lynching at the Fair grounds. Then the front page leader, with its half a column of head-lines caught her eye:

*"EXTRA, SEVEN O'CLOCK"*

*"The Mystery of the Dahomey Village deepens as
the Investigation Progresses"*

*"The French proprietor avers that there was no
attempt at Cannibalism, but he cannot
make a coherent statement
of the case"*

*"The supposedly bloodthirsty Dahomey men and
amazons, said to be the most peaceful and mild
in Africa. The natives contradict themselves and
tell a dozen different stories. The Exposition
management greatly alarmed, and the investigation
being pushed with vigor. Horrifying disclosures
supposed soon to be reached"*

She read it over, then she read it aloud to sorrowing Uncle Jeremiah and Aunt Sarah. The truth of the great unintended hoax and misunderstanding began to dawn upon them. Then she explained the situation, and Johnny was brought out to hear it fully discussed. It was now clear to all of them, but what should they do was the next question. They could not think of the newspaper notoriety that the avowal of the truth would give them. Anyway, it had gone too far for them to interfere. Surely it was wisest and best for them to say nothing. It was so decided. As ludicrous as it was, it had become too grave a matter for amusement.

"Of course you will help us keep this secret, you girls?"

Not a word was returned but Mary picked up her chair and sat down in front of the four girls.

"The noble and progressive association, C. C. of C. C. will now come to order."

Instantly each girl sat prim and upright in her seat.

"Is there any question before this deliberative body of girls?"

Nannie arose and said, "Madam President, I believe it is proposed that we add another secret to our list."

Leila had her note book out and was taking down the minutes of the meeting.

"Believing that this should be done," Nannie continued, "I move that what we have heard and now know concerning this newspaper sensation we forever keep secret."

Stella seconded the motion.

Here Kate got the floor and said she did not think it advisable to add another secret to their list for she now had so many that it was making her life a burden in trying to remember them every time she had occasion to open her mouth. Besides the case would certainly be a scoop for them against the boys and would make them famous and cause the "Weekly Express" to be circulated all over the globe if it published the first true version of the case.

**"THE NOBLE AND PROGRESSIVE ASSOCIATION, C. C. OF C. C."**

There was a sharp discussion for a few minutes, in which parliamentary usage was dethroned and confusion seemed to rule but they were young women and therefore had not lost a word.

The vote was taken and there was but one voice in the negative. There was a motion to make it unanimous and it was unanimous. Thus the wish of their hostess prevailed and another great secret was forever closed In their hearts from the common herds of mankind.

# CHAPTER XIII

## SUNDAY AND CONSCIENCE

Johnny could scarcely wait for nine o'clock of the next morning to come around. He wanted to see if his friend Louis was really alive and if he would be at 60th street gate.

Louis was there dancing about in a fever of anxiety. At John's appearance the two boys went off to talk about their mishaps. They had achieved more adventure than they had bargained for.

"Have you seen the papers?" said Louis.

"Yes."

"Have you told anybody yet?"

"No, and my folks thinks it's best never to say anything about it."

"Then we never will."

"Say, Louis," said John confidently, "there was five of the alfiredest best looking girls around at our house last night you ever saw. Fanny found them at the Beauty show a looking at the sights. They live in a town not very far from our farm and they are coming over to visit Fanny before they have to go into school. You have to come down and visit me while they are there or I will have to live in the barn."

The agreement was closed and the boys passed through the gates in quest of new adventures, as if nothing unusual had ever occurred to them.

However, they instinctively avoided Midway Plaisance, and decided to see what was on Wooded Island. They ranged through the hunter's camp, through the Japanese Hooden, and all over the island in the vain attempt to find something equal to their educated fancies of fun. Somehow Louis learned that there was to be a religious dance in the Quackahl cabin. Nothing else could have a place in the boys' minds until they had tickets for the show.

Inside the hut was a strange sight. Wanug had arranged four of his warriors on the east side of the hut, and these formed a quartet that produced the music for the fearful dance to follow. In the center of the hut a log fire burned briskly. The warriors had their faces smeared with Indian ink, and some of the beauty spots looked like demi-semiquavers on a sheet of music. The squaws, and even the papooses, were painted for the occasion, and everyone of the Quackahls were dressed in blue robes, ornamented with striking pearl buttons.

At a signal Hammasoloe suddenly sprang on the boards and began the mythical movement known as the cannibal dance. It was symbolic of a curious legend current among the Indians of Vancouver island, of a strange spirit that dwells among the mountains and spends most of his time eating the fat members of the Quackahl tribe. Hammasoloe took the part of the spirit and crouched down as if ready to spring on his prey. The sticks beat hard on the plank, and the music for the dance began.

A squaw pounded on a square box, which represented the Quackahl drum. Two warriors were deputed to watch Hammasoloe while he circled around the fire, for the usual ending to the dance is startlingly realistic. Usually the dancer becomes so excited that he bites the arms of those present in imitation of the actions of the great spirit on the mountains. Whenever his eyes glared and his looks became ferocious the warriors grasped his arms and quieted him. He disappeared behind a white curtain, and a few minutes afterward out sprang another warrior wearing a huge mask, representing a raven's head. The raven is a slave of the spirit and is supposed to be represented by one man.

But Awalaskaius played the part of the raven. His body proved as supple as a professional contortionist. He twisted his legs and whirled his head around and snapped his jaws in a remarkable manner. Cries that made the ears ring accompanied the dance.

When Awalaskaius had finished, Hammasoloe sprang out from behind the white curtain wearing a blue gown on which the figure of the Quackahl sun was worked. The rays of the sun were blazing red, and the man in the orb was depicted winking in a gracious manner.

Louder grew the noise, and the quartet taunted the spirit so much that he again disappeared. Then came forth Awalaskaius with a duck's head mask, which is the sign of the great spirit. Again he went through his curious contortions and scared some of the ladies, as he snapped his beak dangerously near them.

When the dance was done and the boys were once more outside they were quite satisfied with sight-seeing among savages and were quite contented to spend the remaining days of the week among the more prosaic and poetical scenes of the great Fair.

Uncle and Aunt had about walked themselves down in their sight-seeing, and were now enjoying the comforts of the rolling chairs and listening to the voluble information which the chair pushers thought it their duty to impart.

Fanny was walking near them in a never ceasing enjoyment of people and scenery. As they passed the Woman's building a large number of women were seen coming out together. On going over the viaduct two well dressed men from the Emerald Isle could be heard in critical conversation.

One of them said:

"Look, Pat! It's women again! Do ye mind that now. Look at um coom out ov that new building. It's the Fair that's bein' run by thim faymales. Soon they'll want to run the wurrld, and they'll be votin'. The divil will be to pay in a man's home. They should be taught their places at once. If my wife should git that strong minded sure I'd be packin' her off. Dacent homes are bein' ruined, Pat, and soon there'll be no homes. They meet in clubs to worship the rich, and who will do our mending and cook our meals? It's all wrong, all wrong. The wsmen must be taught their places."

**"VOLUBLE AND PERHAPS VALUABLE INFORMATION."**

And the poor man looked worried. He is probably teaching Bridget her place today.

Aunt was looking wistfully over toward Wooded Island as if it reminded her of home.

"I tell ye, I haven't saw anything as nice as them flowers. They tell ye of the country, and its quiet over here. Ye get too much of a good thing sometimes out among the white buildings. It's sort o' dreamlike over here, ye know."

She was right, it is dreamlike and it is restful. Din and noise are far away and nothing breaks the stillness but the faint music as it floats down from the plaza. The azalias are in full bloom, and orchids and pansies and nearly every other blossom meet you at every turn.

They stopped at a place where a number of people were looking up at the roof of the Liberal Arts building. Countless small black specks could be seen moving along the roof. Then it was perceived that those specks were really men and women. It is only by such a comparison that they could realize the vastness of these buildings.

"What a jumble of bigness all this is!" Aunt exclaimed, "them people look just like flies on the ceiling or swallows on the peak of our new barn."

The chair pushers took them slowly through Wooded Island.

"What was that, Fanny, that you used to tell me about Alladin and his wonderful lamp?" said Uncle. "I keep a thinking' of that story every time I try to picture all these things at once. Here is fifteen acres of fairy land just like in the fairy books I used to buy for Mary."

They then went on with the crowd past the Government building and the Liberal Arts hall to the basin. On the viaduct, over behind the Statue of the Republic, they stopped to look over that never-fading picture there presented to view. Over the peristyle were written some of the sayings of great men. Fanny read one that heightened the scene into a thrill of thankfulness and patriotism: "We here highly resolve that government of the people, by the people, and for the people, shall not perish from the earth."

"Now," said Aunt. "I believe I know the meaning of this vast expenditure of money and energy. It is not only to show us and others that we have not all the brains; that we are not doing all that is done, but to teach us mutual gratitude for the great privileges of our republic, and fix firm the resolve in the breast of every man that our government of freedom and conscience shall live forever."

They went on out to the pier and dismissed their chairs for seats in the cool lake breeze, where they could see the people coming off of the steamers and approaching them down the long pier on the moving sidewalk.

Wearied with the constant commotion in which they had never been before, it was decided to return home and to spend the remainder of the week in rest and recuperation for another struggle with the world of culture in Jackson Park.

When Sunday came. Uncle was told that the Fair would be opened for visitors. He had been so busy sight-seeing that he had not read the papers or he would have known better. He did not know just what to do on that day, whether to go to church, or the parks, or the Fair, but he was anxious to see what the Fair looked like with most of the people promenading the streets all in their Sunday best. He came to Chicago to see the sights and seeing sights never appeared to him to be wrong. Every Sunday it was his custom to go out into the pasture and look at his jerseys, congratulate himself on how fast his herd was increasing, and contemplate the prospects for the future. Grass grew, the birds sang, the cattle bellowed, and nature was as bright on Sunday as any other day. Besides he had some neighbors who believed that Saturday was the holy Sabbath and he had never been able to disprove their arguments. He believed on general principles that the Fair should be closed on Sundays and that the grass ought not to grow, but since the grass did grow, he would profit by the increase and if the Fair was opened on Sundays, he would not miss its magnificent object lessons.

"Ah, Jeremiah," said Aunt, "every one of them big buildings comes over my spirit like a prayer and when I go inside I see the answer and the benevolence of

God. To shut people out is like padlocking the orchards on Sunday, and stopping the machinery that makes the apples grow. Six days are the rich men's days and God made the Sabbath for the poor. Because our neighbor raises hogs and eats pork it is none of our business because we raise Jerseys and drink milk. The Good Book says: "Let no man, therefore, judge you in meat, or in drink, or in respect of any holy day, or of the new moon, or of the Sabbath days.""

They concluded to go back home and then stroll out, and in their walk to go into the first church they found.

They did so, and came into a great church just in time to hear the minister read the text: "And God said unto Jonah, Doest thou well to be angry for the gourd? And he said, I do well to be angry, even unto death. Then said the Lord, thou hast had pity on the gourd, for which thou hast not labored, neither madest it grow, which came up in a night and perished in a night; and should I not spare Nineveh?"

Uncle Jeremiah listened for the story of Jonah and the gourd to be applied in some way for a lesson to the hearers, but only once, when the minister told what he had seen in Palestine, did he become intelligible to Uncle. It was all so transcendently ethical. Uncle got a remote idea that Chicago was to be likened to Nineveh, and the gourd to the World's Fair, but when the sermon was done, and all said, he felt that he would have enjoyed the hour so much better in some of the quiet shades of one of the parks, where he would have heard so reverently the still small voice of nature's teachings.

After noon they went to Lincoln Park, and as they stood before Lincoln's statue, Aunt said: "This is greater than any sermon I ever heard." They read the words and sat on the bench encircling the statue, while Fanny read the sayings of Lincoln chiseled on the stone. Then they visited Grant's monument. They sat down on the stone steps and looked at the noble figure. Uncle was carried away with a religious patriotism that held all the emotions of divine presence.

## "THIS IS GREATER THAN ANY SERMON I EVER HEARD."

"There," said Aunt, "we are listening to another sermon that can not be surpassed by the tongues of men. A whole life of great deeds for our country is here speaking to us. No man can be a bad man if he were to come every Sunday and give his emotions up to the lessons of the lives of Grant and Lincoln. Divine emotion is not aroused alone by words from the pulpit or the silent walls of a house. Seeing is as great a means of God as hearing, but seeing receives its sermons from the infallible; hearing listens to that which may come only from the brain."

**"THE POLICEMAN CAME OUT OF THE BOX AND WALKED RAP-
IDLY DOWN THE STREET."**

It was late in the afternoon when the four of them got off the cable car at Monroe and Dearborn streets and walked leisurely toward their hotel. At one of the street corners they saw a policeman come out of the patrol box and walk rapidly down the street. In a moment more he was joined by three other policemen from another street. Uncle turned to watch them, when suddenly they began to run, then faster, almost as in a race.

"Sure they're going to arrest somebody," said John, and he started after them at break-neck speed with visions of a murder probably being done just around the corner. Uncle became excited also and started after them followed by Aunt and Fanny, not knowing what else to do. Uncle and John reached the corner breathless and looked each way to see where the robbery or murder was being done, but what was their disgust to see the three policemen climbing into a cable car and calmly taking a seat. It was an outrageous sell on all of them, but it could not be helped, and there was no law by which they could sue the policemen for a false alarm. They had the right to run to catch a car if they wanted to. The family went on more deliberately now for they had no breath to spare and there was but little to be said. Uncle felt that Chicago was very much of a mockery anyhow. But he had seen enough to make him desire to see more.

The tremendous puffing and blowing of a tug was heard somewhere in the river and they concluded to go over to the bridge and see what it was. There was a mystery anyway about how those big boats got past the bridges.

Uncle and Aunt walked on over the bridge but John and Fanny stopped to hear the music made by a cornet band of girls on one of the excursion steamers. The tall masts of a lumber boat could be seen coming rapidly toward them in tow with an insignificant little steamer. There was a jing-aling two or three times of a bell hid somewhere in the framework of the bridge, teamsters and people were hurrying across, and all at once the bridge began to move. Johnny saw some people remaining on the bridge and catching Fanny by the hand he cried. "Here let's take a ride" and in a moment they were swayed past the street and out over the stream. Over at the other end they saw Uncle and Aunt holding desperately on to the railing. They had not been able to get over when the bridge moved away. Presently the boats were past and the bridge rapidly swung into place. Down the street half a block Johnny saw some steam issuing from the middle of the street. Instantly the idea of a volcanic eruption in the middle of Chicago possessed his mind. He called Fanny's attention to it and their curiosity was greatly excited. They had heard that Chicago was a very wicked place and their preacher had once remarked that he would not be surprised at any time to hear of an upheaval by the Lord sending the city over into the lake. In considerable dread lest the overthrow was about to take place, they walked towards the place along the sidewalk, as the famous Harry walked up to the guidepost at the country crossroads on that cloudy night so long ago. But they were greatly reassured when they found the people about them were so indifferent and they were chagrined to learn that they were again deceived. It was no volcano, there would be no terrible cataclysm, it was only an inoffensive man-hole to the sewers, into which the waste steam of one of the factories near by was escaping.

Meanwhile, Uncle and Aunt had stepped off of the bridge and were intensely bewildered all at once to find that the excursion steamer and the houses next to it had all apparently jumped across the river to their side.

"Did we come acrost that bridge?" Uncle asked.

"I know we never."

"How did we git acrost without coming acrost?"

"I can't see how anybody could come across without comin' across, and I know we never," said Aunt.

"Well, ef we hain't acrost, then the houses are acrost, and it is more natural fer us ter be crazy than for the houses to get acrost."

"Ask the policeman."

Uncle went up to the policeman and said: "Say, Mister, we want to know if you will be so kind as to tell us ef we are acrost or not acrost."

"Do you mean on the north side or the south side?"

"No; I mean on this side or the other side."

"Well, which side did you come from?"

"I thought I came from the other side," said Uncle, "but it seems now as if I came from this side and didn't go over to the other side at all."

"Where have you been?" asked the policeman, making a mighty effort to untangle himself.

Uncle was becoming impatient.

"I tell you I've been acrost that river 'cause I walked acrost, and then I never walked acrost again, and here I am not acrost, and I want to know how I got back acrost again."

"Say, old lady!" said the policeman, "ain't he crazy?"

"This is the first time I really ever thought so. We've been seeing too much, and I guess we're both crazy."

"In that case," replied the officer, "I am compelled to take charge of you."

"O Grandma!" cried Fanny, just then running up, "ain't this great. Johnny and I have been nearly half an hour trying to figure out how we got across the river, and I found out first. You see the bridge just went straight half around, and so when we got on this end here it carried us around to the other side and carried you back around to this side."

"Bless the Lord!" said Uncle, fervently; "Sarah and me ain't crazy yet, and the policeman needn't worry himself." But the policeman was gone.

"You see, Fanny, we couldn't make it out, and Sarah and me and the policeman all agreed that we was stark gone daft."

Uncle and Aunt now had enough for one day, and they heartily wished they were back on the farm. But they swallowed their discomfiture: and, after a good night's rest at home, determined to visit the Board of Trade, where Bob Simmons had lost the fortune his father left him.

**"IS THEM THE FELLERS THAT THE FARMERS IS AFRAID OF?"**

Uncle and family did not get around to the Board of Trade till nearly eleven o'clock the next morning. There was a wide entrance with a stairway on either side. Uncle saw the people in front of him, and he was accustomed to pass right in among the congregation and take his seat in the amen corner. He did not notice that the others had stopped at the door, but he plunged right ahead. The door-keeper evidently had his attention engaged at something else, for he let Uncle walk on in. Some one at the door spoke to the ladies and told them to take the left stairway to the gallery. They reached there just in time to see Uncle in a difficulty below. A young man had him by the arm and was pointing very vigorously toward the door.

"Who do you want to see, sir?"

"I want to see the Board of Trade. Where is it?"

"Go outside and up the stairs into the galleries and you can see it all you want to, but not here."

Uncle did as he was bid, but found that he was quite widely separated from his family, because he had been sent up the opposite stairway from them.

"I came up to see the Board of Trade," he said, confidently, to a well-dressed stranger next to him.

"Well, there it is in all its glory," said the stranger.

"Oh, I see! The board is that table where them fellers is a tickin' them machines. You see I thought they would be a setting and a trading across a long, wide board like they used to do at the country stores for counters. But them fellers down there acts like a lot of lunatics. I don't see how they can ever come to a bargain, yelling and spewing around that way. And then I don't see the bulls and bears that change the market."

The stranger thought it a useless job to try to enlighten him.

When Uncle and his family came down, he went up to the doorkeeper and asked, "Say, do you belong here?" The keeper nodded. "Did you know Bill Simmons what lost five thousand dollars here last year?" The door keeper shook his head. "Well, say, I just want to ask one more question. Are them people down there the bulls and bears themselves, and are they the Board of Trade and are they the people that the farmers are so afraid of?" The keeper nodded.

"Well," continued Uncle, "I've got this to say; any set of farmers as is fools enough to be afraid of them yelling idiots, aint got no backbone at all."

Chicago was unsettling many of Uncle's ideas, and he began to decide that the only real, bonafide thing he could swear by was his own farm, and that the great outside world was only a great circus of art and extravagant genius.

# CHAPTER XIV
## SIGHT-SEEING GALORE

Under promises of gorgeous sights and full protection, Fanny had concluded to visit the chief Midway Plaisance theaters with Johnny and Louis as escorts. The "Midway," as it is familiarly called, is undoubtedly the most unique and interesting pleasure-walk in the world. It is a thoroughfare of ever-shifting scenes and ever-recurring incidents. Fanny was not sure she ought to go, and Johnny could not comprehend why she did not go with him as readily wherever he proposed as she did on the wild free life of the big Jersey farm. But this was to her a supremely different existence, and she tried hard to recall all she had seen and heard and read of etiquette and the proprieties. Uncle and Aunt were not the only ones who were bewildered at every step by the amazing mixture of reality and art, of fact and fancy, of nature and imitation. They felt as if their souls were living apart, and that they were mere automatons in a panoramic world.

Johnny had seen the Soudanese and Nubian play actors just before his disastrous attempt to be informed concerning the Dahomey village. But some scoffers from the South had spoiled part of the novelty of it by alleging that the men of northern Africa were really natives of Mississippi or Louisiana, and were dancing only plantation hoe-downs in slow time and increased perpendicular action.

But without question the high histrionic art of the Chinese, Javanese, Turkish and Algerian actors ought to be seen. Maybe it was strangeness rather than excellence and novelty rather than entertainment that drew the people but strangeness and novelty are the greater excellence when people come to see wonders.

The Chinese theater is by far the most pretentious. It was pretty well advertised to the world at the advent of the actors in Vancouver and their encounter with the custom officers. They came to Chicago several hundred strong and are housed in the big blue-and-gilt structure with trim pagodas near the Cottage Grove end of the Midway. Entrance to the theater is through a big tea house, where decent-looking Chinamen who do not look like rats and whose fluent English proclaims their long sojourn in "Flisco," serve the cheering cup at from 10 to 60 cents, according to the pliability of the victim. They are doing a business worthy of a better cause. The tea house is but the ante-chamber to a joss house overhead, mendaciously advertised to be "the biggest outside of China," and to the theater proper. The latter is not so big as the Chinese theaters in San Francisco, but it smells sweeter, being over ground and not surrounded with the cooking-rooms and opium bunks of the actors. This is a concession to occidental taste which all but oriental enthusiasts will appreciate. Nor are visitors allowed, as in San Francisco, to inspect the green-room or sit on the stage.

**"SHE VISITED THE PLAY AND SINCERELY REGRETTED IT."**

In other respects the theater is pure San Francisco Chinese. There is the orchestra, led by the man with the yard-wide cymbals, playing the leading part. There is the property man, always in evidence, who places a chair and says "This is a horse," or turns the chair around and calls it a mountain. And there is the female impersonator with deeply roughed cheeks, who is the pride and flower of histrionic art. Women are not allowed to walk the boards of the Chinese theater, but the male actor who best can mimic woman's tones and mincing airs is the Henry Irving. There is a whole chorus of these men-women in the Jackson Park theater — an all-star combination. As for the piece itself, they first play a little curtain-raiser of about two-months' duration and then the real play occupies the rest of the year. It will be all one to the American visitors, however, who enjoy the novelty, so that they are allowed to quit when they like. And there is no objection to that from the polite Chinamen in charge of the Jackson Park theater.

The Turkish theater is across the way and farther east than the Chinese. It is back from the beaten path and you might miss it — if you were deaf. Having ears to hear you will be apprised of its whereabouts at forty rods distance by the orchestra, which sits on the front steps and discourses horrors on a sort of flageolet and a bass drum. The orchestra plays only one tune and it plays that hard. When a respectable house has been gathered by these out-of-door allurements the curtain rises on a Turkish play. It is a sweet pastoral of a youth who is lovesick and cannot be cured by the doctor, by the soothsayer — by any one except his love, who comes in time, and there is a wedding.

When this play was ended, Fanny decided that she had seen enough of foreign theaters and declined to go further.

A Boston girl in spectacles sat near her through the Turkish play. She told Fanny that she and her mother had been venturesome enough to visit the other plays, and they sincerely regretted it. She found a mongrel horde of Turks, Arabs, Europeans, blacks, Greeks—everything applauding an interminable song, whose filthy motif it needs no knowledge of Arabic to discover. The singer was an Algerian woman, good enough looking, after the pasty style of oriental beauties, young, agile and mistress of the curious, droning guttural melody which constitutes oriental music. She plays her part with complete abandon, probably because she knows no better, and her audience applauds her wildly for the same reasons. The Boston girl said she had seen these same girls, or their professional sisters, in the Algerian theater. But their performance had been modified to suit the western taste. They sing and dance, but their songs and dances are nothing more dangerous than a languorous drone. But there are also some funny parts, according to the Algerian idea. They are played by a jet black Somauli woman who joins in the dance and a jet black Somauli boy in the orchestra who has a face of India rubber and a gift for "facial contortion" that would make the fortune of an American minstrel.

**"FACIAL CONTORTION THAT WOULD MAKE THE FORTUNE OF AN AMERICAN MINSTREL."**

A look at the outside of the Soudanese theater is enough for the ordinary curiosity-seeker. It is a little round hut of bark in a dark corner of the Egyptian enclosure. Mahomet Ali sits at the receipt of custom exchanging pleasantries with dusky flower girls whose home is by the orange market beyond the Kase el Nil, who know more French than English, and more deviltry than either; who sing "Ta-ra-ra Boom-de-ay," and know how to solicit backsheesh to perfection. The theatricals here are simplicity brought to perfection. It is said their language consists of only a hundred words. If you were to paint your face black, look wild-eyed, stiffen your hair in many strands, array yourself in a cotton garment that revealed more than it concealed, and then were to jump straight up and down to the music of a dolorous chant you would not be far astray. Add to this a whining and interminable appeal for backsheesh and you might be very near the mark indeed. But there is one Soudanese performance you could scarcely hope to equal, unless you were to learn some sort of devil's chant, gird your loins with a loose belt of shells and by rapid contortions of your body make these primitive cymbals accompany your chant. This is the star of the troupe.

Romantic people, who like to think of dancing as the poetry of motion, can get a liberal education in muscular poesy by making the rounds of the Midway Plaisance. They may see sonnets in double-shuffle metre, doggerels in hop-skip iambics, and ordinary newspaper "ponies" with the rhythm of the St. Vitus dance. Slices of pandemonium will be thrown in by the orchestras for the one price of admission, and if the visitor objects to taking his pandemonium on the installment plan, he may get it in job lots down at the Dahomeyan village.

In their "dance," as it is termed, they take a step forward with the right foot, and drag the left after it. This is repeated until they stub their toes on the orchestra, when they swarm back and go through the difficult feat of advancing by a series of hops on one foot. All of this is to the discordant pounding of drums and scrap-iron, where tune could not be discovered with a search warrant.

That evening Fanny visited the C. C. of C. C. and arranged for a family picnic at Washington Park the next day. She was to be hostess, and they were to have an outing with her in the city's artificial fields and forests that would recall the merry life of the country, and yet they would be surrounded by all the artistic embellishments that money and genius could secure.

Johnny went post haste for Louis, and the two boys were made bearers of the lunches, guides of the expedition, the vanguard of the march and the responsible protection of the company. They were eight merry young folks who took possession of the grip-car on the Cottage Grove Avenue cable line that morning. They stopped at the park hot-house and spent two delightful hours in the wilderness of flowers and of palm forests. On the outside were rustic seats about a pond where, in waters made tepid by steam heat through iron pipes, all kinds of tropical plants flourished in a profusion perhaps not excelled anywhere on the equator or along the banks of the Amazon. The great flower clock and the immense flower globe showing the geography of the earth, the old English castle gate and the carpeted lawns showed them the skill of the gardener's art. A quiet nook was found near the water's edge of one of the ponds. With a newspaper for a table-spread they enjoyed a lunch where hunger was a sauce better than Worcestershire, and the sod a better resting place than a throne.

After their lunch and a good rest they returned to the business part of the city and spent the remainder of the day in the Mystic Maze, the Labyrinth and the Panoptican. These were places where electricity and mirrors were arranged with the object of reversing every conception the eye had ever given to the mind. In one place the visitors entered a triangular room in one corner of which there was a large vase of flowers. The walls were solid mirrors and the six girls found themselves as if in a host of people and a wilderness of flowers. From this they passed on into a room which the attendant said was forty feet square and contained thirty-eight mirrors six feet by eight set at different angles between posts evenly distributed about the room. As they stepped forward they found themselves among countless hordes of people, again they were alone, all at once they found themselves in a line of girls that stretched on either side apparently for miles. One time they would be brushing around among people about two feet high and two feet thick; again they would be surrounded by thousands of girls eight or ten feet high and correspondingly thin. It was exasperating to say the least. When they became weary of this novelty they looked about them for the attendant but he had mysteriously disappeared. Leila said she knew the way out and she started with all the confidence that a usually level headed girl can have, but alas! she nearly broke her head by running into one of the big mirrors. Nannie happened to look in a certain direction when she saw the door and the curtains about it as plainly as she ever saw anything in her life.

"There I see the door," she cried, "come this way," and she started with her hands out before her like some one feeling his way in the dark, though it was as bright about them as the electric lights could make it. All at once the door she had in view disappeared like magic and she stood before herself in a mirror ducking her head backwards and forwards like two young chickens with their beaks just touching in the preliminaries of a fight. The situation was becoming too serious to be amusing any longer.

"What shall we do?" said Fanny, who had read of death in the mysterious labyrinths in ancient times. The roof was low, and even if the sky had been their roof they had no wings, like Daedalus, whereby they might escape.

The girls began to get nervous, and several million of them seemed to huddle together as they discussed the situation.

"I say, let's yell!" said Mary.

"But what is the use to yell," one said, "if they have determined that we are to die here?"

## "THEY HELD TO ONE ANOTHER, AS IF FOR LIFE OR DEATH."

Now they were becoming really frightened. The picture of their lingering death in that frightful crowd of specters was most horrifying. Their voices were becoming tremulous and hollow, and the terra-cotta figures of wild Bedouins that sat in a niche of the far wall and was multiplied a thousand times, seemed to grin at them maliciously, as if in anticipation of seeing their agonizing struggles against death by hunger. The suspense was becoming something terrible.

"I say somebody must yell."

"Let Kate yell, she's got a strong voice that might reach the street."

Kate tried to do her duty, and she said, "Oh, Say!" in a voice that would not have wakened a rabbit from its slumber.

She tried again, "Oh, say, we want to get out!" in a voice so hollow that none of the girls recognized it as hers.

"Is ze ladies seen eet all they want?" said the polite attendant, as he seemed to come before them at one step.

"Where were you?" they all cried.

"Why, I vas by ze glass about tree feet away."

"And you were listening to all we said?"

"Oh, I do not leesen. Eet ese my beesness to go out weeth you ven you ask eet."

And then they followed him out.

"What a horrid place that was and we thought at first it was so nice," said one.

"In all our lives we can never have a dream half so frightful as that was," said a third.

"One thing sure," said Mary, "this terrible experience has bound us forever and forever together; and because of our common experience in this awful adventure we must initiate Fanny into the mysteries of the noble order of progressive girls, C. C. of C. C."

# CHAPTER XV
## A TERRIBLE EXPERIENCE

Foreign theaters, mazes, labyrinths, panopticons, spectatoriums and their ilk had no more charms for the girls, but with Uncle and Aunt they spent the next day in the museums, casinos and panoramas of the city. But wax figures and brain-muddling deceptions were still the value they received for their money.

"I will be contented," said Aunt, "never to leave the farm again. I can be happy there the rest of my born days in knowing that when I look at a cow it is not a stuffed cow, that the calf by her side can move; that the man on the barn floor with his pitchfork in the hay can really lift it over into the manger for the cattle. This mornin' I see a lady standin' on one of the stairs tryin' to tie her shoes. She was having a time of it, I knew, so I says, says I, 'leddy, let me help you.' She didn't say nothing, so I jest stooped down to help her. I pulled the tongue of the shoe up and tapped the sides together over it, when a perfect chill came over me, for I pressed the lady's ankle, and it felt just like sawdust. Poor woman! I thought some terrible accident had cut off her leg and she had a false one. I looked up into her face, and she looked so pale like and deathly that I was awful scared, then I looked more and more and I see she was dead, died maybe of heart disease while she was a stooping over. O what a shock! I can not get over it to my dying day. I nearly screamed but I knew I must not, so I just called to the feller sitting at the table writing visiting cards to come there quick; but he just set there stock still and never moved. I didn't want to attract attention from the folks around so I just picked up a nail a lying there and hit him square on the cheek but he never flinched. I spoke then to the woman leaning over the railing laughing at the little girl down below but she never changed her smile at all. I couldn't tell what to make of it when a feller came up to me an' says, 'Do you want anything, old lady?' I stared at him and says 'Hist, sir, don't you see this poor woman is dead. Died a stooping over too sudden.'"

**"SO I SAYS, SAYS I, 'LEDDY, LET ME HELP YOU.'"**

Then he just laughed at me a little, and pulled her dress to one side and showed me that she was only a wax head and a stuffed body. That made me mad, for it is a sin and a shame for to deceive people that way, and defraud 'em of their hard earned money. I told him to show me the way out, and I would report how he was defrauding the public to the humane society or somebody. He just laughed at me again and invited me to take a chair in the office if I wanted to wait for my folks. I went in there and an awful nice woman talked to me and explained things till I wasn't so mad as I was; but I still think it is a shame that a Christian city should allow such awful frauds on peoples' eyes and nerves. Anyhow, when I get home I want to go around and touch everything and make sure that there is no more foolin', so I can live in peace and facts."

Aunt was very indignant. She could stand the deceptions that Uncle had been so opposed to at the Fair, but when she was deceived in her acts of kindness, it was carrying things entirely too far.

The places of interest, as the guide books said, had now all been visited, and they were walking down the street fully satisfied that they had seen all the sights of the city from the skyscrapers to the organ grinders. The police courts and the stock yards were not considered as places of interest by them.

John and Fanny were in the lead, with the five girls just behind them, and Uncle and Aunt bringing up the rear. As they reached the corner there was a clamor and a scattering of people crossing the street, and a rumbling that jarred the earth as two great fire engines dashed by rolling smoke upward and clanging a bell in a way that was frightful.

"Fire, fire!" shouted Johnny.

"Oh that's what we want to see, a fire, a big fire," echoed the girls.

In a moment they were all running pell mell after the engines, jostling against the people and exciting the merriment and wonder of every body. The engines were running in the direction of their hotel and very likely it was on fire and they would lose all their clothing.

"Come on girls," shouted John as he led the way like a foxhound. "Come on, I know it's only just around the corner. I see the smoke rolling up from the house."

The engines had turned another corner and Johnny felt a great pride in being the guide and encyclopedia of ready information for six girls. Out of breath they reached the corner where they supposed they would see a terrible fire with people jumping out of the windows twelve or fourteen stories high, perhaps safely into blankets, possibly to their death. Or, brave firemen scaling ladders and bearing lovely girls out of the horrible flames. But they discovered that the smoke they had seen was coming out of a tall chimney, and that far down the street almost a mile away they could get glimpses of the fire engines still forging straight ahead. But they were not to be daunted thus. There must be a great fire somewhere down there that it would take many hours for the engines to get under control. On and on they ran, out of breath, to be sure, but determined to see the great Chicago fire that required two such great engines to bring under control. They had run several blocks, when they became so tired they could only walk. Another block or two was traversed, when they met the engines coming leisurely back. It was a bitter deception, there was no fire. They turned back; and, when they met Uncle and Aunt, also entirely out of breath with the chase, Aunt declared that this was only another case of Chicago's base deceptions. It could joke with dead people and jest with fires and make a playhouse exhibition costing many millions of dollars, and fool old people and the young alike and with equal conscience.

Uncle observed that it proved to him that Barnum was right when he said that a fool was born every minute, and that the Americans were a people who delighted in being deceived.

The girls decided to remain that night with Fanny, and to visit the Fair together the next day. A pleasant evening was spent, but the subject of fire and fire escapes were the chief topic of conversation. Each of the windows of their room had a fire-escape fastened to the facing, and the instructions printed underneath were carefully studied and mastered by all before retiring.

The next morning they were gathered in the main room awaiting the time for breakfast. Johnny raised a window to get a look outside, when the well known clang! clang! clang! of the Chicago fire engine was heard. Instantly all was excitement. Clang! clang! clang! and another came by. Then there were two or three more, and they seemed to stop right under the window. People across the street, even up to the top stories, were complacently sitting in the windows and looking into the street as if such a thing as great flames lapping upward and smothering them to death, were unknown. Johnny, who was looking out of the window, yelled: "O Lord! it's our house on fire, and we are five stories high!"

The streets began to fill with people. Uncle, panic-stricken, looked out and saw the engines puffing below. The cool audacity of the people at the windows across the street was appalling. They did not care for death. All at once Uncle recovered himself and yelled: "Everybody to the life preservers! Git into the fire escapes and save yourselves!"

But the room was empty. "Oh Lord," Uncle groaned, "they have gone insane and run down into the flames below."

Wringing his hands he ran to the door and cried, "Oh Sarah, Sarah, come back and let us die together." But neither Sarah nor the rest were anywhere to be seen. He was alone.

Remembering the instructions regarding the fire escape, he ran to the window, fastened the straps about his waist and climbed out of the window. He pulled the string that was to unreel the rope and let him down. Down, down, he went expecting every moment to feel the fierce heat about him. He seemed to be half way down when the reel ceased to work and he hung there suspended in mid air awaiting an awful death. He gave a despairing jerk when down he went within three feet of the pavement with a sudden stop that took his breath away. A crowd of people began to gather about him.

**"HE HUNG SUSPENDED IN MID AIR, AWAITING AN AWFUL DEATH."**

"What's the matter old man," said a man who had seen all the performance.

"Where's the fire," said Uncle wildly.

"It is two blocks further up," he answered.

"And ain't my folks all burnt up?" he said pathetically.

The answer was at once before him for he had let himself down directly over the entrance of the hotel and his family just then arriving at the bottom of the stairway came out to him. There never was a more happy meeting for Uncle than that one. His ridiculous adventure was not clear to him till he had time to study it over. But there really was a fire further on and they were not to lose such a sight.

**"THE FIRE WAS TWO BLOCKS AWAY."**

A large dry goods house was on fire, and eighteen or twenty monster engines were puffing and roaring, each one like a threshing machine on Uncle's wheat field. They pressed themselves forward to the very front of the spectators, and so close that the heat of the flames could be distinctly felt. A heavy wind was blowing, and all the force of the fire department was out to stop the flames. It was truly the grandest and most fearful spectacle the family had ever seen. There came a puff of wind toward them and the flames came down, almost scorching their clothing. Then the policemen commenced to drive the crowd back.

**"SOMETHING HAPPENED."**

There was almost a panic, and the girls nearly had their lives crushed out of them. It was an adventure they cared never to repeat. Johnny did not fare so badly, for he was more intent on the workings of the engines. He was free from mishaps till he chanced to take a position over the great hose-pipe through which the water was sent with such tremendous force on its mission. Something happened. He is not able to relate just how it was. But the hose burst directly under him, and he was tossed over into the streaming gutter with a precision he can forgive but never forget. After this happened it was time to go home to be more agreeably clothed. Johnny was a sadder though a wiser boy.

# CHAPTER XVI

## TO BUY A DOG

Jackson Park was a paradise of peace and rest compared with the nerve destroying difficulties of sight-seeing in the city. Uncle had experienced all the adventures he wanted, and his great desire now was to escape all further mishaps until he could get back safe among his Jerseys on the farm.

Tired from much walking among the scenes of the Exhibition, the family sat down upon one of the rustic seats in Wooded Island. It was a most picturesque place, a most inspiring spot from which to contemplate the great sweep of history that had culminated on those grounds.

"The longer I stay about this Fair," said Uncle, "and the more I see, the more I wish I knew. I can see folks discussing things with such great delight when I can't understand anything but the ifs and ands and buts. I heard a man say to-day that Columbus never discovered America, that he was a pirate. He said that all these doings should have been for a Viking or some such name. I knew it wasn't so, for so many people couldn't be fooled. How may that all be, Fanny?"

"There are a great many theories and stories set afloat about the discovery of America by people who desire more to show off their ability to construct plausible heresies against accepted things than to give real historic truth. But there is much that at least seems to be evidence of the Norsemen having been in America 500 years before Columbus touched the outlying islands of the West Indies. The Sagas of Leif the Lucky and Eric the Red told some marvelous stories of discoveries to the southwest of Iceland. Some of these stories seem to be verified in many ways, by digging up the logs of the Norse huts, by the written characters on Dighton rock, by the old tower at Newport, by the Benheim map of 1492, and a number of other important things.

"Then there has been found what seems to be beyond doubt a figure of Buddha in Yucatan, and also a Buddhist monument in Central America. Therefore a number of people have been trying to prove that Hwul Shan of China, discovered America ages ago. There are likewise well established the claims of the Phenicians and Greeks and even the Welsh and the Irish. But all of these were fruitless till Columbus in his high aspirations to become a great prince over unknown countries and to spread the Christian religion of his day, opened the way for the course of Western empire."

"But Fanny," said Uncle. "I heard the man say that Columbus didn't know anything and had no chance to learn."

"Yes, Father, this glorious year has taught to the students all over this country the beginning history of our great republic even as this Fair is teaching the progress of the world. Though Columbus was the greatest man of his age, yet we know only that he was the son of a wool comber and that he attended the school at Pavia, where he showed a marvellous aptitude for astronomy and cosmography. He became a sailor on the Mediterranean, some say a pirate, but the ships of one nation then preyed on the ships of another and considered it legitimate because there was then no International law. He married the daughter of an Italian named Palestrello, who had been a celebrated Portuguese sailor. With her he received many valuable charts, journals and memoranda. He soon moved to Lisbon, which was then the center of everything speculative and adventurous in geographical discovery. Columbus made a living here by making maps. Here he studied out his theory that he could reach Asia by going west, and he made several voyages to the Azores and Canary islands, which were then the limit of sea navigation. Then began his travels for help to carry out his wonderful plans. He took with him his motherless boy, Diego. From place to place he went with a heroism of patience never surpassed. The story of the rebuffs and privations through which he passed will be the wonder and praise of men forever. Weary and footsore and hungry, he stopped one day before the Franciscan Convent La Rabida, in Andalusia, to beg some bread and water for his child. Then came the mysterious turning of the scales in the forces of human greatness. The Superior of the convent happened to pass by, and, struck by the appearance of the poor traveler, began to talk to him. The Superior at once saw that no ordinary man was before him. Grander views were never presented and greater plans of conquest were never known. Christianity was to invade Asia on its eastern shores and meet the irresistible forces from the West. Columbus believed himself divinely inspired for this and therefore demanded that he be made high-admiral, governor-general and viceroy over all the land he reached and that for his revenue there should be given one-tenth of the entire produce of the countries. Such a far reaching demand as this could not have been acceded to only by a doubting sovereign, and he would probably have been beheaded with his puny crew of one hundred and twenty men if he had reached Asia and attempted to carry out such a wholesale scheme of subjugation.

"The months of this voyage were scarcely less full of treason, burdens, and peril than the years that had been given to make the voyage possible. A pension was promised to the man who first sighted land but Columbus saw a light rising and falling on the evening of Oct. 11, and on that account claimed and received the pension. It is said that the sailor who really saw land first foreswore his country and fled to Africa because of having lost the pension and the honor of being the first to see land. This is told by the enemies of Columbus to prove a sordid and avaricious nature. It is also told that he took such exasperating and outrageous measures to uphold his visionary schemes of conquest and government as high-admiral, governor-general and viceroy, that it became more than his home government could endure.

"His last voyage was disastrous, but whether from his own desire for gold hunting, or because from the demands of his crew, it can not be told. A man was sent to supersede him and chains were placed upon the man who had worn the robe of royalty. His last years before the public were even more bitter than his first. Until his death he seemed to spend all his time in trying to recover from the king his lost prestige, titles and possessions, but they never came. He besought Ferdinand pitifully to bestow them as a perpetual heritage upon his son, even if not to him. In a letter to his sovereigns, he said: 'Such is my fate that twenty years of service, through which I passed with so much toil and danger, have profited me nothing; and at this day I do not possess a roof in Spain that I can call my own. If I wish to eat or sleep, I have no where to go but to the inn or the tavern, and I seldom have wherewith to pay the bill. I have not a hair upon my head that is not grey; my body is infirm, and all that was left me, as well as to my brothers, has been taken away and sold, even to the frock that I wore, to my great dishonor. I implore your highness to forgive my complaints. I am indeed in as ruined a condition as I have related. Hitherto I have wept for others: may Heaven now have mercy upon me, and may the earth weep for me!'

"He died in bitterest poverty at Valladolid at about the age of seventy years. He was buried at Valladolid for a short while to satisfy the Franciscans, and then removed to Seville by request of his relatives. It was said that Columbus wished to be buried in San Domingo, and Charles V. gave authority for this to be done to the grandson of Columbus, and the family of Colon was to occupy the chapel of the cathedral. But there is no record whatever of the events of his burial at San Domingo. This is accounted for only on the theory that Drake, the English pirate, destroyed them when he sacked San Domingo.

"In 1795 Spain ceded San Domingo to France and it seemed to the Spanish people to be a national disgrace for the bones of Columbus to remain on foreign soil. There were no explicit directions as to the exact spot where his bones were and it was not known then that five of the family were buried together there. What was supposed to be his ashes were taken to Havana but in 1877 while making some repairs in the vaults another tomb was discovered in which was a strip of lead from a box which proved that the place contained the ashes of the grandson of Columbus. Then a further search was made; only a few inches from the vault first opened another vault was found and in it a lead box containing pieces of bone and human dust and on the lid was written

*"D. de la A. per Ate"*

which is supposed to mean "Discoverer of America, First Admiral." A silver plate inside had inscribed on it the names and titles of Columbus. This much decomposed leaden case was placed, with its contents, in another case of satin wood and glass, and all deposited in a vault so that the contents could be seen through the glass. Spain could not think of giving up the honor of having the bones of Columbus on her own soil, and the Royal Academy of Madrid made an exhaustive study of the subject and at last published a book in which they closed the argument with the following words: "The remains of Christoval Colon are in the cathedral of Habana, in the shadow of the glorious banner of Castile. It is most fit that over his sepulchre waves the same flag that sailed with him from Palos in the Santa Maria."''

After reviewing this history, which her interest in the great Fair, and the great events it commemorated, had caused her to learn, and after consulting her note book to be sure of her correctness, there was a general discussion among them, which showed that sight-seeing was not all they were doing at the Fair.

**"SOME BODIES FOR THE HEADS AND FEET."**

It was now past noon. Aunt decided to go home; Fanny would walk up and down the "Plaisance," and with her sketch book see what she could do toward putting bodies between some of those heads and feet she had drawn. Uncle and Johnny decided to go up to the business portion of the city to spend the rest of the day. It was a pleasant afternoon, and when they reached the viaduct from the train a great mass of people were passing and repassing. The great Auditorium building loomed up before them, with the Art Gallery on their right and the Columbus statue on their left. Under them trains were gliding by like long serpents, and out in the lake fleet steamers and sail-boats loaded with people were moving about like white spots on the blue waters. Uncle and Johnny passed along the sidewalk in front of the hotel when something at the corner caught their attention, and they came up for a moment to look at it. Two or three men also turned, stopping by him when he stopped. Then a few more came up, and a ring of men began to form. Uncle and Johnny now noticed that they were surrounded by people, and they attempted to move out, but in vain. In a short time the crowd had become so large that the sidewalk was blocked, and none except those who were close to the center knew what the original attraction was. The people coming over the viaduct and from far down the street noticed the crowd too, and bent their steps also in its direction. Some, fearful that they would miss something, began to run. The contagion for speed spread, and soon the whole mass were speeding up the boulevard with open mouths and wide-staring eyes. Each was asking the other as he ran, "What is it?"

As they came in contact with the central surging crowd where each man and woman was trying to see over the heads of those in front, despite the fact that the object, whatever it was, was on the ground, the question was repeated. But no one seemed to know what had happened. People in the center of the crush began to demand room and air. In vain they struggled to get out. The people still coming over the viaduct would start into a run as soon as they were on the street, and thus continually adding pressure on the outside made the positions of those inside almost unbearable. The crowd was now a pushing, clamoring one, extending some distance up and down the sidewalk and out into the street. The apparently insolvable mystery as to the nature of the accident or cause of the excitement only made the crowd more persistent and harder to manage. There were some who shouted, "give the poor fellow more air." "It's a shame to crowd around him like that." Then they would push harder than ever to see what it was.

Two men pushing each other got into an altercation. One struck the other, almost knocking him down. The crowd quickly took hold of the injured man and shoved him out into the "outer darkness," as if he had been a criminal, while the other was let alone. Some shouted for a doctor, others for the patrol and ambulance and the police. At last two officers came. After ringing up the patrol they forced their way through the crowd, which quickly fell in behind them and pressed on again with the renewed hope of seeing something. The presence of the officers only added to the general excitement, and people who had been

laggards or had left in disgust came back at a double quick.

When the police got to the wall of the building they found a man who had two Newfoundland pups tied to a string. The patrol wagon was sent back empty, and the crowd, which had been sold instead of the pups, dispersed.

When Uncle got out he took his bandana out of his hat and mopped his forehead, as if he had just finished tossing up a load of hay to Johnny on a hot day in the hayfield.

**"ONLY A COUPLE OF NEWFOUNDLAND PUPPIES."**

"Consarn them critters!" he said, "I was thinkin' of buyin' one of them Newfoundland purps for Fanny, but the crowd was so anxious to see the trade that I've got entirely out o' the notion. I never see such curiosity people in all my life. The other day I stopped at a winder, and before I got half through seeing there were about fifteen people standin' around and lookin' over my shoulder. I guess I can't see anything any more without tollin' so many folks on that I'm liable to get crushed. If country folks was half as curious 'bout things as these city folks, they might be laffed at with some sense."

# CHAPTER XVII
## CAIRO STREET

"And so you call this the Anthropological building?" said Uncle. "What kind of things has it got inside to have such a name?"

"Well, Grandpa, if you desire to be enlightened scientifically, I may say that it is a subject beginning with Adam and including the whole human race. It is divided into five parts: zoological anthropology, showing the differences and similarities between men and brutes; descriptive anthropology, showing the differences and similarities between the races; general anthropology, which is the descriptive biology of the human race; theological anthropology, which concerns the divine origin and the destiny of man; and ethical anthropology, which discusses the duties of man to the world and his creator."

"Do tell! it's a pretty big subject, and no wonder it has a house to itself."

Inside they found skulls, skeletons, bones, savage relics consisting of dress, utensils, ornaments and weapons with amulets, charms, idols and everything pertaining to early religions the world over.

On the eastern border of south pond was to be found the outdoor ethnographical exhibit. Indian groups, Indian schools and everything illustrating their primitive life and material progress.

There were objects, shell heaps, village sites, burial places, mounds, cliff houses and the ruins of Mexico, Central and South America. To see the same thing, and to only very little better advantage, would require thousands of dollars and years of perilous travel.

"The more I go through these places," said Uncle "the more I feel ashamed that I did not do my share in bringing of relics. Now I could have brought the old nightcap that sister Susan's dead husband's grandfather brought over from England; and I have a gridiron that my great aunt gave me to remember her by. And there's the snuffers and the old wood-yard rake that my grandfather made himself way back in New England, and the dress in which my aunt Harriet was married, and the horseshoe from the foot of the horse that killed cousin John's boy Tom, and sister Hanner's gold fillin' of her tooth, which was the first gold fillin' in our parts, and it came out just afore she died, and I don't know how much more. Ain't they anthropological, ethnographic biology or something like that?"

"I think, Grandpa, they would have been more useful in some kind of a cabinet in the old settler's cabin, but we needn't to fret about it any."

From here they went over to the Midway Plaisance. The "Street in Cairo" was to be opened with a great parade of some kind and they wanted to see it. The natives call it *Mars-al-Kabia*. In fact the Street in Cairo was all the curiosities of Egyptian Cairo's streets crowded into one Chicago Cairo Street. It was a splendid sight with its gardens and squares, its temples, its towers and minaret made in the most Arabesque architecture and ornamented with the most fantastic draperies. The inhabitants had been directly transported from old Cairo across the sea to Midway Plaisance. There were the importunate street venders, the donkey boys begging and pulling at the clothing of the visitors, the pompous drivers of camels beseeching the visitors to try their "ship of the desert;" tom-tom pounders, reed blowers, fakirs, child acrobat beggars, Mohammedans, Copts, Jews, Franks, Greeks, Armenians, Nubians, Soudanese, Arabs, Turks, and men and women from all over the Levant, all in the gorgeous apparel of the East, filling the booths or strolling about the street. They were the happiest lot of Orientals that ever got so far away from home. Drums were beating, camel drivers singing merry songs, and a curious medley of voices which the earth beneath them never heard before. At eleven o'clock somebody blew a strange kind of horn, which made the small boy almost kill himself in his frenzy to get near to see what it meant.

Musicians mounted the camels and began grinding out music that was enough to frighten even a North American Indian to death. At the first glimpse of the camels a team of steady old horses, that probably were never frightened before, ran away with the gravel wagon which they had been patiently dragging along. Little Arabs and Soudanese ran ahead of the procession turning somersets and clapping their hands in hilarious glee. There were warriors hopping about and clashing shields and swords together in mimic battle. In front of Hagenbeck's show the lions were aroused from their slumber in the den above the entrance, and they stood before the bars and roared at the procession. Then the dancing girls came skipping along, followed by a bride and her maids, for at last it was seen to be a bridal procession that was celebrating the opening of "Cairo street" in Chicago.

## "HURRAH! IT HUMPS IN FRONT, JUMPS BEHIND, AND PACES IN THE MIDDLE."

Here is the circus of the "Plaisance," where the visitors are the actors and the clowns. Every hour can be seen a bevy of pretty girls escorted by a brother or some dapper young man. The camel drivers hail them. What a chance for a lark! "Let's have a ride on the back of the queer creature," says one maiden. "Oh! you wouldn't dare," replies brother. "Wouldn't I, though? Just watch me," is the modern maiden's response. She approaches the dromedary, which opens one eye by way of recognition. She passes silver to the hand of the dark-skinned menial. The other girls giggle. A great crowd gathers round to see the fun which experience has taught is coming. Now the bold young woman is in the saddle, and holding tightly, as advised, to the strap which hangs near by. The dromedary opens the other eye, shuffles his rear and longest legs in the dust with a sound that resembles the hum of an approaching cyclone, gathers himself for an effort, and suddenly presents to the gaze of all beholders a rear elevation notable for its suddeness and its altitude, if not for its architectural beauty. Though catapulted about ten feet higher than she had had any idea of going, the American young woman does not scream. That would be unbecoming woman in this woman's era. She merely presses her lips tighter together, lets her smile fade away at the corners of her pretty mouth and grasps the strap as if her life depended upon it. The crowd, of course, laughs.

By this time the dromedary has shuffled himself some more along the brick pavement and opened the ugliest mouth ever seen this side the Nile. Now he shows his front elevation, and the smile which had returned to the lips of his fair rider fades again as the other end of the animated catapult is put into operation. But only for a moment. The bystanders have only begun their second laugh when the American young woman is seen to be herself again. She is out for a good time, and she is having it. The dromedary winks three times and puts a sinuous, sway-ing sort of motion into his body. His fat feet and angular legs begin to describe semi-circles. The saddle and its rider twist and gyrate and revolve and stop short, only to start quickly off again in some other direction, and the triumphant journey through the "Street in Cairo" has begun.

It is a very narrow thoroughfare, this oriental street, and it has no sidewalks. The crowd falls to either side. As the courier of the desert humps through the lane made open for him, his rider is seen smiling and happy. She knows she has a pretty foot, and that it is neatly clad in red shoes with tapering points and the most becoming of hosiery. She knows her figure is trim, and that her cheeks are bright and her eyes flashing. Applause follows her from the mosque to the temple of Luxor, and rolls back again as her beast turns for the homeward march.

She has had a ride on a real dromedary, caused palpitations in a hundred mas-culine hearts, and made 500 of her sex envy her the possession of such feet, figure and nerve. But these are not her sweetest triumphs. The consciousness to her most grateful and satisfying is that the courage and the independence of the modern young woman of America have been exemplified and vindicated.

They must get their fortunes told. There were no gypsies in this Cairo such as camp along the country roads or in the edges of the villages and tell sighing swains about their loves. Here was a seer imported direct from the banks of the Nile.

His father studied the stars and read lives from the palms of men's hands. His grandfather did the same. He came from a race of wise men. The first seers of his family sat in the shade of the early sphinxes and told Egyptian maidens to beware of young men who came up from the Red sea with false promises.

But his fortune-telling was of the same kind as one finds everywhere. A young man paid the price and held out his hand. The wise man took hold of the fingers, bent them back from the hand and pushed the cuff half way back to the elbow. He traced the course of the veins, ran his coal-black finger along each wrinkle of the palm, and all the time muttered to himself. Sometimes he nodded his head and gurgled approvingly. Again he hesitated and groaned feebly, as if the signs were sad. The young man had a scared look in his eyes. Then the interpreter began to tell what the aged seer had to say:

"He says that you had sickness. It was not long ago. You were afraid. But it's all right. You won't be sick any more. Have health, good health. Feel good all time. Don't be afraid."

"I'm glad to hear it," said the young man.

"Before you worked where you do now you had another kind of work. You did something else. You will change. Not the same kind of work next time. No, no. You will have good time. A man will give you work. It is different from what you do now. He is short, fat, very rich man. Go with him. You will do well, make money—lots of money. Fat man will make you have better clothes."

"Well, what's the matter with these I've— —," began the young man, but the interpreter hushed him.

"He says you must stay in Chicago, good place. If you travel you will not have as much money as you will have when you get with the fat man. You must stay here if you want to be rich and have good clothes. Aha! this is very good. Put your head near. He says you are very warm-hearted, like all of the women. Yes, yes, that's it, you love one in particular, your wife or some one. He wants to know who it is you love."

"I am not married," said the young man.

"He says," resumed the interpreter, "that it's all right."

"All right, eh?"

"Yes, you will marry her, but not this year."

"How long do you think you will live?"

"Give it up."

"You will live to be 87. He says so."

That was all, and the puzzled young man arose to go away.

"How was it? How was it?" asked all the women who had been looking on and marveling.

"I'll tell you," said the young man. "The past and present are both a little cloudy, but the future is all that any one could ask."

Then he started away, keeping a sharp lookout for a fat man who seemed to be rich.

At the end of the street is the Temple of Luxor, where the curious pass under the deity-covered portal, and gaze upon the reproduced wonders of ancient

Egypt. They bend over withered mummies of kings dead 5,000 years ago, and listen to music that has not been played for ages.

Near here is the passage way outside, and, as Fanny came out with her ears ringing with the strange jargon that everywhere met her, she was at once relaxed from the tension of sights and sounds she had just been in by seeing two country people rush together just before her. One said:

"Well, what in the world are you doin' here?"

"I swan, is that you? What are you doin' here?"

"Oh-h-h, we had to see the Fair, couldn't miss it, you know, not if it took a leg."

"That's right, that's right. Bring your folks?"

"Oh, yes, they're around here somewhere. Mother's about fagged. Says she'd rather cook for harvest hands than walk all day. Going to stay long?"

"Calculate on being here all next week if body and soul stick together. 'Spose you'll be here sometime."

"Can't tell yet. Just about give up seeing it all. Half the time don't know whether I'm on my head or my heels. Blamedest place I ever struck."

"That's right, that's right."

It was enough to cause her to smile at their homely enthusiasm, and the striking contrast of language. It was a relief to hear intelligible language once more, and in the rural dialect so familiar to her ears.

The soft, balmy days of June were now in their glory, and Uncle and Aunt sometimes spent nearly the whole day sitting around on Wooded Island imagining they could hear their cattle lowing in the pasture across the creek, and dreaming their lives over again from their early happy days. It was so peaceful there. Then they loved to go over by the lake and look upon it as a painted ocean, as calm and quiet as a pond of Raphael. It was something to see the stretch of blue go on till it touched the low-hung clouds at the edge of the world. Beyond the mists and the smoke of the white steamers were dimly outlined streaks of yellow and light, which turned the whole heavens into a softened sky of good promise. In the foreground of the vista the giant figures of victory, with charging horses and chariot, and all the Apollos and Neptunes, stood out like silhouettes. There was no noise save the ripple of the water down the cascade at Columbia's feet. Gentle winds lapped the waves along the beach, the furious breakers of other days were toned into a delicate murmur, which sounded very like some sweet symphony or the hymn of a winged choir. Waves which had for weeks been tangled masses of white caps and had thrashed with frantic anger the bases of the towering pillars dropped to the dainty ripples of a summer breeze. There was no crash, no roar, no splashing spray, driven on by a gale that snorted and snapped. So delicately and silently did the waters kiss the shore that sparrows and wrens and a flock of wandering doves walked to the very edge and filled their crops with the pure white sand. Then this, the best great work of any race of any age, comes over the spirits of worshipful men like heavenly benedictions of good-will and peace.

Sometimes as they sat in some quiet place alone saying nothing but thinking joy, the music of holy melodies came floating across the waters of the basin and re-echoed from the heaving lake to the Administration dome. They were sitting at the feet of that human genius which God had hallowed for the sake of those who revere His holy name.

They were everywhere thrilled with the supremely gifted achievements of their fellow men, inspired by the living canvass from every clime, and amazed to know that the lumps of Parian stone could be made to speak the heroism of the world.

# CHAPTER XVIII
## UNCLE IN THE LOCK-UP

Our family felt that they could remain in the grounds forever and never be done seeing; but the time was drawing near when they must return home. Uncle decided that this Saturday must be their last day at the Fair. Surely they had seen enough, even if there was so much more not yet seen. They had seen notable people all the way from the Infanta of Spain to Faraway Moses, of Egypt. But they were all the same to Uncle. He had heard all kinds of music, from the Spanish band to the Samoan tom-tom. "Some of the music," he said, "was so peaceful like, but the rest was not half so nice as the growin' pigs rubbin' against splinters in the sty back of the barnyard." He had surely been all over, and there was nothing more of a startling nature to see. He had watched them check babies at the children's building as if they were poodles or handbags, and he had been over to the Irish village and seen the people kissing the "Blarney Stone." On a card tacked near by he read:

> *This is the stone that whoever kisses*
> *He never misses to*
> *Grow eloquent.*
> *A clever spouter*
> *He'll turn out an orator*
> *In Parliament.*

Uncle had no ambition that way, and so he let the rest do all the kissing.

He had completed his sight-seeing in the city by taking a Turkish bath, and he considered himself now ready to "pull up stakes" and return to the farm.

"I've made hay in July, and punched it back into the loft," said Uncle; "I've harvested in August, and drunk out of the branch; I've cut hoop-poles in the swamp, and done lots of other hot things, but fer real sultuy weather nothing is ekal to the Turkey bath. Some feller told me it was the healthiest bath a feller could take when there was no creek around. You see, I looked at the Chicago river and decided it wasn't altogether a proper place fer a swim; then I went over to the lake whar they were a paddling around, but somehow the water didn't warm up even a little bit in the afternoons, and then I thought I might just as well pay a dollar and take a Turkey bath.

"Well, it do beat anything in the wash line I ever see. I went into the barber shop where the sign was and paid a woman a dollar, and she took my silver ticker and chain and all my spare change, and my pocket book, and put 'em all into a box and locked it and then fastened the key around my wrist. Well, I wondered if I was a going down there whar they had to protect me that way from getting robbed.

"I went down stairs where I stopped to see a feller a doing some thing to a feller's feet. I seed he was a cutting the nails, and then I thought how awful lazy these city people do get, that they can't even cut their own toe nails.

"A feller came up and put me in a little room and told me to strip off and foller him. Well, sir, that feller he just stuck me into a room that was hot enough to fry eggs and bake Johnny cakes. I dassent breathe hard for fear of burning my nose off. He set me into a lean back chair and decently covered me over with a sheet. I've biled sap, an' I've rolled logs; I've scraped hogs over the kettle and made soap, but this beat anything I ever see fer hot weather. If I hadn't seen other respectable folks goin' in there I'd a knowed I was a gittin' basted for my sins in the bad world. I couldn't set there, so I tried to walk around, but I seen my feet was liable to get roasted, and the air was hotter at the top, so I set down again.

"Well, sir, I sot there till I got hotter'n biled corn, and then I hollered worse nor the Johnnies at Kenesaw mountain.

"Then a feller stuck his head in at the door and told me to come out there, and when I did a colored feller shoved me on to a bench and began to slap the daylights out o' me with both hands, and then another feller he turned the hose on me, and then I cut loose.

"Well, sir, you ought to a seed me. I'm gittin' old, but 'nough is 'nough, and I kin be painters an' wild cats when I want to. I was in a pecooliar place without a stitch on me, but I jest run the slapper into the bake oven, and I made the buggy washer jump into the fish pond or swimmin' hole what they aimed to chuck me into next; and then a feller came out and took me into another room, where he rubbed me down kind a horse like, and I got my clothes on and went up to the woman and got my things give back; and I told her I was awful glad to see daylight again. She laffed, an' I didn't say no more, but I done lots of thinkin'.' "

They were sitting on a rustic bench, just across the southwest bridge on Wooded Island, when Uncle's talking was brought to a stop by a great noise in the direction of the "Plaisance." Just then two Turks came trotting by with a sedan chair in which was seated a nervous-looking woman who seemed anxious to reach the place from which the medley of noises seem to be issuing. She nervously grasped the sides of the chair and looked at the bent form of the toiling Ottoman in front. Over the bridge they went, the carriers executing a double shuffle diagonally down the steep descent. The passenger opened her mouth and gave a scream that made the Turk in front stumble as he bent his head to see what was wrong. Then she screamed harder, frightening a flock of sea-gulls off the island and bringing a Columbian guard on a run from the north entrance of the Horticultural building to see what was the matter. Then she insisted on getting out, and she was so glad, that she gave the Turk a dollar, and left before he could give her any change.

## "SHE GAVE A SCREAM THAT SCARED SOME GULLS OFF OF THE ISLAND."

The noise over towards the "Plaisance" continued, and Johnny cried out, "The parade, the Midway Plaisance parade! Come on, the whole earth is parading!"

The front of the procession just then appeared in view, and the family went to the top of the bridge where they could review the strangest procession that ever walked on the western world. Processions may come, and processions may go, but there never was one like that which was then winding through the broad streets of Jackson Park.

The column was over a mile long, and made up of men and women afoot; camels, gaily decked horsemen, wild Bedouins from Arabia's desert's; carriages, rolling chairs, reindeer and dog sledges. From the fur garments of the Laplanders leading the column, to the sea-grass, thoroughly ventilated costumes of the Samoans, was presented a contrast that marked the display all along the line. It seemed as if there had been a revival of the Babel scene from the Pentateuch. It seemed that the confusion of tongues had just come to pass and people had not yet become accustomed to talk anything but Sanscrit or Chinese.

There was a gathering of assorted freaks not surpassed since Noah came out of the ark, and an assortment of people never seen before. When Mr. Moody preaches to the Midway Plaisance, surely the scripture will be fulfilled as to preaching the gospel to all the nations of the earth.

Then the bedlam of strange cries were heard again. These peculiar sounds came from the Dahomey warriors and amazons, black as night and stupid as pigs. In thin cloth and hair garments that concealed just a little of their bodies, the blacks romped as they sang and beat upon long cartridge shaped drums.

The noisiest part of the parade began with the Algerian village. Drums resounded, clarinets screeched, castanets clattered, and the shrill cries of the dancing girls rose above all the tumult. The girls rode in rolling chairs, and while they were not busy rivaling the banshee of Ireland, they laughed and flirted to their hearts' content.

The Chinese was the most gorgeous contingent in the column. Costumed in rare and brilliant silks, ablaze with gold and silver, the Chinese actors and actresses made a brilliant appearance. But it was the dragon that wriggled behind them that caught the crowd. It was 125 feet long, and its mouth was big enough to swallow a man without tearing his clothes on its fangs. When it passed the beer tunnel in the "Plaisance," its glaring eyes turned toward a man whose best friends have been to Dwight. The man shuddered and drew a long and nervous breath.

"Take me away from here, Bill," the man said to his companion. "I never thought I could get in this kind of a fix. I'm a quitter right now."

From a distance it looked like a monster sea serpent on a spree. It was really a dragon, at least that's what the Chinese call it; but it was in fact the finest exhibit ever beheld of what a diseased imagination can do for a victim of strong drink. It could easily claim the prize as being the most terrifying object on earth.

The people from the "Street of Cairo," afoot and mounted on camels and donkeys, headed their part of the procession with the Turkish flag, and swift-footed runners guarded the banner, while men in rusty, antique chain-armor were near to defend. A horde of fakirs and jugglers of all colors, from jet-black Soudanese to fair-faced Greeks, pressed close at their heels, stripped to the waists, with bare feet, and cutting up all sorts of tricks. Swordsmen, garbed in long robes, twirling naked blades and shields as they hopped about one another in imitation of combat; more donkey boys; Nubians bearing carved Egyptian images, one of which was of the sacred bull done in gold; bayaderes and nautch dancers, not very good looking, but with fine white arms and well-turned ankles and gorgeous in oriental robes and colors—all flocked after the fakirs.

Then came the Persians, the women playing upon hurdy-gurdies and singing a plaintive air more suggestive of melody than any other native music in the line. The lion banner of the Shah was carried proudly, and this detachment closed with a score of Persian gladiators, naked to the waist. They seemed to be superbly executed pieces of bronze set in motion.

The "Beauty Show" was in the parade. Blarney Castle had several lads and lasses present, led by the pipes and a jig-dancer as agile as an antelope and as tireless as an electric fan, for he jigged all the way the procession marched. Then the Samoans came along. Stalwart men are they, yellow-skinned and muscular, and in their airy sea-grass garments, knee short and chest high, they presented a splendid physical appearance, while the women were pleasant-faced and fairly pretty. The men danced a war dance while marching along, and their fierce wielding of their clubs had greater influence in putting back the fast encroaching crowds than did the oft repeated command of the Columbian guard to stand back.

The South Sea Islanders, with nothing much more than feathers and grasses about their bodies and on their heads, sang a wild but tuneful melody as they brandished war clubs and danced about, their well-greased bodies gleaming in the sun. Three pretty Hula-Hula girls in the party sang all the time. Their dress was very fantastic; short, full skirts of brilliant-colored grasses fell to their bare brown knees. Flowers and grasses were twined in their hair. A short, tight-fitting robe of grasses and feathers fell over their shoulders and ended at their waists.

The young women who illustrate all the various types of beauty to be seen anywhere on earth, from Hong Kong to State street, made up the line. They were in carriages, and attracted much attention.

The odd procession traversed the Fair grounds to the east end of the Electricity building, and then returned to their respective shows.

It was now getting late in the afternoon and Uncle said, "Now, let us be taking our last looks."

"Papers, Mister? All about the Sunday Fair."

Uncle bought a paper and read the headlines:

*"GATES REMAIN OPEN"*

*"Courts' Final Decision in Favor of Sunday Fair*
*Judges are Unanimous — Overrule Judgment*
*of United States Circuit Court"*

*"Court Room and Halls Crowded with People*
*Eager to Hear the Decision"*

*"The Chief Justice brushes away the Cobwebs of*
*sophistry and religious paternalism by which the*
*Sabbatarian sects sought to close the Gates*
*against the Millions"*

"I didn't see no millions when I was here Sunday, did you, Sarah? And the grounds looked lots like a big grave yard, with some people sad like, a wandering through."

The sweat began to come on Uncle's face. His big bandanna was brought into play. "So they've opened it. Well, I don't know, I don't know. It kind of worries me somehow, as if they oughtn't a done it. But I don't understand all the law and the gospel. I surely didn't do no wrong when I thought seeing the Fair on Sunday was right, if it do disturb me like, just now. I thought our Savior meant seeing the Fair on Sunday when he said 'It is lawful to do well on the Sabbath day.' But when

I see the beer tunnel full of people, and the furrin theayters a runnin', it didn't look lawful, and I wisht I was back to our old church a sittin' in the corner. Anyhow, I hope I didn't do any of it."

Uncle walked on slowly in a very sad and meditative mood. Aunt looked as if there was something that had overthrown all her high sentiment on her first Sunday of seeing the entrancing visions of the great Exposition. There were religious realities touching her soul now, and she walked on rapidly with Fanny, leaving Uncle behind. Johnny was flipping pebbles at some ducks in the lagoon and Uncle had stopped to look in at one of the doors of Liberal Arts hall. While he was standing there two dapper young men came walking hastily by. One caught sight of Uncle and quickly uttered a low whistle. His companion stopped short as the first one said: "Der's de old duffer; let's work him."

"Naw, we can't do it. He'll remember me mistake in change an' de blasted trainboy biz."

"'I'll bet you a fiver he don't! You're trigged out altogether new, an' your gran'mother wouldn't know ye."

"Nothin' like tryin', so here goes," and the speaker walked on a few steps and half concealed himself behind a column, close enough to hear all that was said.

"Well, how do you do, Deacon Jones? I am awfully surprised. It's like two needles meeting in a haystack for us to meet here. Isn't it now! It's a long time since I saw you back in old Barnville, Sage county, Indiana; but I remembered you the minute I clapped my eyes on you. I suspect you'd like to hear from some of your old neighbors."

The speaker was still holding Uncle's hand, and Uncle was looking at him in a bewildered manner, as if searching intensely in the picture gallery of memory's old time faces.

"I see you can't place me, but I guess it's 'cause I was only a chunk of a lad, but I see you often in the 'amen corner' of the Barnville Baptist church. You see my father was killed in one of the battles before Atlanta, and mother and me, when I was a boy, didn't have much to live on, only our pension. So I had to work hard, and didn't git around much for to be seen by anybody. I was converted and joined the church just about the time you moved away. Then I went into Mr. Monroe's store and got to be chief clerk, and then when the bank was opened at Barnville I was made cashier, and in three or four years I was called to be cashier in the First National here, so you see I have been more successful than most of the poor boys about Barnville whose fathers never came back from defending their country."

**"I SEE YOU CAN'T PLACE ME."**

"Ah, my boy," said Uncle, "my heart always warms up for my comrades' children. I believe I recollect you now. Wasn't you the boy what swum out into the crick at high water, when the bridge went down while preacher Barker's wife was crossing with her baby to bring him back from Bethel, and towed 'em safe to shore?"

"Yes, sir. I'm the lad."

"Widow Brown's son George?"

"Yes, sir, George Brown, from Barnville, is what I am."

"Well, well, my boy, I knowed I recollected you. My memory's bad enough, but I haint forgot ye and yer brave deed. Well, I'm glad your succeeding so well, and I hope you haint forgot your redemption before the Cross."

"No, Deacon, I haven't, and I trust I am doing the Lord's will, as I ought, though I know sometimes I fall short. I take part more than most of the young people in our church, but I trust I will still be moved to do more and more for our holy cause."

"There, there! It's proud I am to see in this great wicked city one of Barnville's boys so true to the teachings of our Lord and Master that he learnt in our old home church."

Here the young man coughed lightly, as if the emotion of religious memories was swelling up in his throat and almost choking his utterance.

"But I guess everybody has forgot me at Barnville. It's mor'n twelve years now."

"Not at all, Deacon. Every time I go back there to the old church I hear somebody speak of Deacon Jones."

"Do tell——!"

At this moment a young man came up hurriedly and tapped "George" on the shoulder. "George" turned at once, and said: "How do you do, Henry? Henry, this is my old friend, Deacon Jones, from the home of my boyhood. Mr. Jones, Mr. Wilson. I am proud, Deacon, to have you meet my friend here, who is one of the Exposition directors and manager of one of the most important departments on the grounds."

"I would be very glad to talk longer with you and your friend Mr. Brown, but I was just hunting for Johnson, the paymaster. Iv'e got to have two hundred dollars inside of ten minutes or there will be the biggest howl among employees you ever saw."

"Oh, you needn't hunt any longer for Johnson, Mr. Wilson, here's my check for the sum and you can cash it at once at the World's Fair bank," and Mr. Brown, who was none other than Arthur Blair, the confidence man and bogus detective, drew out a First National bank check book.

"But that's exactly the trouble. It is now past banking hours, and for some reason Johnson has not come around."

A troubled look came over Mr. Blair's face in his anxiety to help out his friend. Turning to Uncle he said: "Perhaps the Deacon can help my friend out and then cash my check here on the grounds in the morning."

Uncle looked uneasy for a moment, and then said: "Of course I can accommodate you," and he pulled out a roll of bills and laid aside $200, which left him with only thirty dollars.

Mr. Blair had the check made out and was just extending it to Uncle when Johnny came up, a curious spectator of the scene before him. A second glance at the gentleman talking to his grandfather and he began to jump up and down and whirl around yelling at the top of his voice: "Perlice! fire! murder! robbers! pickpockets! confidence men! thieves! thugs! highwaymen! bandits! outlaws! catch 'em! hang 'em! crucify 'em! here, here, everybody! surround 'em! close in on 'em! let no guilty man escape!"

The two confidence men were for once too astonished to act quickly, but one recovered himself soon enough to make a snatch for the roll of bills in Uncle's hand. Two or three corners of bills were torn away, but Uncle held the money.

In an instant a dozen men were crowding around, and among them two or three officers.

"Catch that old thief!" yelled Blair, "he's got my money." "Catch him!" cried Wilson, appearing to try to get at him, "he's got our money."

Uncle was standing in blank stupefaction holding the bills in his hands and staring at the gathering crowd.

An officer caught him by the arm and said: "Old man, where did you get that money?"

Uncle found his tongue at last, and said: "Mister, I got that from Bill Shaw for some of the finest Jerseys you ever seed."

"Here, officer, are our cards and the charge. We'll appear in the morning at the station."

Johnny had been overwhelmed by the crowd, but by this time he had edged his way in, and when he saw his grandfather in the tolls of the law he yelled shrill enough to startle the whole crowd.

"Grandfather's done nothing, let him alone. Here's the thieving hypocrits." But the two young men had disappeared among the people, and Uncle was being taken away in such a crowd that John could get no view whatever of the situation, so he ran howling and sputtering round and round the fast increasing crowd like a child gone insane. Presently the uselessness of his action made him think of Mother and Fanny. At once he darted off to the spot where he had seen them last, and in his wildness to find them ran past them two or three times, till Fanny saw him and in amazement cried, "Johnny! John! What on earth is the matter with you, Johnny?"

Johnny darted over to them and yelled out: "He's tuk up! The cops has got him! grandfather's tuck up, and he's done nothing, and them bloody bandits got away again. Oh! Oh! Oh!" and Johnny danced around, incapable of telling Fanny or his grandma anything further.

But they learned enough to know that for some reason Uncle had been arrested and was no doubt now in the guard house. Aunt was overwhelmed with consternation, but Fanny ran over to a guard standing near by and inquired: "If anyone is arrested on the grounds where do they take them?"

"Over there to the guard house, Miss. There they go with some old chap now."

### "HE'S TUCK UP, HE'S TUCK UP! THE COPS GOT HIM!"

Fanny looked and could scarcely repress a scream as she saw Uncle seated in the patrol wagon between two policemen. She ran back to Aunt and Johnny and told him to run as fast as he could to see where the wagon went, and they would follow in the same direction. Johnny was off like a shot as he saw the wagon rapidly disappearing over the way.

Out of breath they were coming up to the station door when they met Johnny, hat off, and almost speechless with excitement.

"They've took Grandpa's money and everything, and locked him up. They asked him if he had any friends, and he said he had no friends here but us. Nobody listens to me, come quick," and he started them off on a run for the station. Arriving there, the officers in charge told them he could do nothing for them unless they could find some responsible persons to secure his appearance for the preliminary hearing of the next day. They were taken around where Uncle was, and a more woe-begone appearing farmer never was seen.

"Ah, children, this is Chicago!"

"Grandpa, I'm going to find Mr. Warner. I believe he is a good man, and will help us, as he told you he would. Johnny and I will start at once to find him. I don't know what else to do."

"But, child," said Aunt, "it's already five o'clock, and the people will all be gone home from the store."

"No difference, Grandma; you stay right here, for we're going."

She took the card from Uncle that Mr. Warner had given him and left the building with Johnny walking resolutely by her side.

# CHAPTER XIX

## THE LOST FOUND

They took a car, and in half an hour were at the doors of the Clarendon Company. It was past business hours and the doors were locked. Fanny was greatly distressed as to what she should do; but there was no time to lose. Some young men were standing near eyeing her with the usual sensual greediness of their kind. Her mission was too urgent for her to notice their insinuating remarks.

"Can any of you tell me where or how I may find the gentleman named on this card?"

Her demeanor, so unaffected and true, brought all their latent manhood out, and each one was anxious for the honor of helping her.

Some one standing in the rear made an unbecoming remark, and instantly the eyes of those about her turned on him so meaningly that he slunk away. One of them took her into a restaurant near by and made known to the proprietor what she wanted. He said Mr. Warner lived with the head of the firm, a Mr. Sterling. The street and number of the residence was given to a cabman, and soon they were driving rapidly away.

Mr. Sterling was sitting alone in his library reading the evening papers, when he heard a determined ring at the door. His door was open into the hall, and he went himself at once to answer the call.

It was growing quite dark, and he could distinguish only that there were two young people standing before him.

"Is this where Mr. Sterling lives?" said one, in a very pleasing tone of voice.

"It is."

**"HE HEARD A DETERMINED RING AT THE DOOR."**

"We are very sorry to disturb you, but we are in some trouble, and a gentleman by the name of Warner told us if, for any reason, we needed any assistance while in the city, to call on him. We went to the store, but it was closed, and then we were directed to come to you in the hope that through you we could find Mr. Warner."

John and Fanny saw a kindly appearing business man before them, and they spoke with the utmost confidence in his good-will.

"So, so! that is good. I have heard him speak several times recently of a young lady he met on the train, and somewhere else once or twice since. Are you the young lady I have been teasing him about? Now, that is good. Of course you can see him. He lives with me and is up-stairs now. May I ask what is the nature of your trouble?"

Johnny could hold his tongue no longer.

"Why, sir, they've tuck Grandpa up and got him in jail 'cause I stopped some crooks a gettin' his money."

"I don't see, my boy, just how that could be," and the gentleman seemed somewhat suspicious of their grandfather.

"I don't, nuther," blurted Johnny.

"Come in. I will send for Mr. Warner and see what he can do for you."

They followed him into the room, and he motioned them to take seats. Then he went out and sent some one up-stairs for Mr. Warner.

**"FANNY, MY LITTLE GIRL—MY LOST CHILDREN!"**

The room was richly furnished, but had an air of negligence about it that betokened the want of an interested woman's taste and care. They could hear voices now and then coming from some distant part of the house, but they sounded more like the hilarious gaiety of servants than of persons having such a cultured place for a home. From the tapestries on the walls to the piano and the great case full of books, everything was arranged for the convenience of the one rather than for the taste of the many. It was the most pleasing home, where money was lavishly spent, that she had ever been in, and perhaps she is not to be blamed that for a moment she was carried away by her surroundings, and the longing came over her to be so happily situated as this. Seeing a life-size painting of a woman placed on a high frame near a desk, she went over to look at it. There was something so lifelike and natural, and even familiar, about the picture that she still further forgot how she came to be there. She did not hear Mr. Sterling as he re-entered the room, but he came up to her, and as she stepped aside the light fell full upon her face almost on a level with the picture in the frame. A startled expression came over the face of Mr. Sterling, which deepened into an amazement. His face grew white, and he looked at her and then at the picture, and then from the picture to her.

The light of some quick intuition spread over her face, and she thrust her hand into her cape pocket and drew out a small gold locket, which she opened and looked at intently, and then from the face of the man to the face of the woman. Mr. Sterling saw the locket.

"What are you looking at, child?" he almost shrieked.

"My mother and father," she said.

He caught the locket out of her hand.

"There, there," he cried, pointing to the painting; "there is the same picture, it is the picture of the only one I ever loved, the one now in heaven, and you are her living image. In God's name, tell me, child, what is your name."

"My name is Fanny," she said, "Fanny Jones; sometimes they call me 'Fanny Sterling.' Mary Sterling was my——"

She never finished the sentence. With a cry of joy he caught her in his arms, sobbing and laughing; "My child, my child, my own little girl; found, found at last!"

Johnny at this amazing outburst had come up as if to protect his sister, and as Mr. Sterling saw him he cried, "And is this your brother, the baby I left never to see again till now?"

Mr. Sterling sat down and drew Johnny up to him. "A rough, hearty, honest farmer boy," he said; "I can not realize that after an endless search, you have been sent to me in such a strange manner."

Mr. Sterling overcome with his emotion, buried his face in his hands, and Fanny kneeling by his side, looked wistfully at him, not knowing what to think or do. Mr. Warner, in answer to the call, had come to the door and witnessed the whole scene. He could not understand it, and his astonishment rendered him speechless. At last without moving from his place at the door, he said: "What can this mean, may I ask? It is a mystery to me."

"My children," was all Mr. Sterling could say.

Her mission there suddenly came back to Fanny. She sprang to her feet and cried: "Oh! Mr. Warner, my grandpa is in trouble. You told us to call on you if we needed assistance in anything. He is in the police station as a result of our acquaintance with that man on the train. I came for you to go with us and see what you could do to help us out."

Everything was soon explained to them all; the cab that brought John and Fanny there was dismissed, and Mr. Sterling's carriage was soon speeding them all to the fastest train for the Fair grounds. At the police station half an hour later there was sorrow turned to joy, and a meeting that was too happy to be told. Uncle was released on bail to appear the next afternoon to answer to the charges, and there was a reunion at the hotel in another hour, when every past ill was forever buried in the pleasure of the present and the promise of the future. The next morning Mr. Sterling's house was made their abiding place, and Fanny became queen of his home.

That afternoon Uncle was in the police court awaiting his accusers. The judge called the case, but the witnesses were not there. Their names were called, but no one answered. Just then two boys came rushing into the room.

"Hold up, yer honnur," said one, "de persecution will soon arrive. I've been after 'em, an' I got 'em. I see 'em doin' de robbin', and' I found a policeman whut had sense enuf to take 'em in. See!"

**"LOUIS CAME IN DANCING WITH EXCITEMENT BEFORE THE BURLY POLICEMAN WITH HIS TWO WARDS."**

The irrepressible Louis had hardly ceased speaking when a burly policeman entered with the two confidence men who had attempted so perseveringly to get Uncle's money. Behind them came the man they had just been trying to rob. Johnny and Louis had seen them talking to a countryman, and, divining what was intended, followed them as they tolled him away to a place where they could accomplish the robbery. They found a policeman on the way, who took in the situation and assisted the boys to catch the fellows in the act.

Uncle's case was dismissed, and Louis succeeded in seeing the crooks given a chance to learn an honest trade at Joliet.

Sight-seeing as a business now gave over to a new order of things. The change was almost beyond what a dream could be. Before the C. C. of C. C. returned home there was a social gathering at Fanny's new home. Johnny had one young friend present and Fanny had five. Mr. Warner had often noticed that Louis was a very reliable boy, and Mr. Sterling gave him a good position in his store. Uncle and Aunt could not part with their children, and Johnny was so thoroughly a farmer that there could be no thought of him doing anything else; therefore, it was decided that Uncle's Jerseys should be removed to Mr. Sterling's farm, half an hour's ride from the city, and that Johnny should have charge of them there. Soon after, Uncle and Aunt sold their farm and henceforth lived as they pleased with Johnny and the Jerseys, or with Fanny in her happy city home. Mr. Warner is trying to win the approval of Fanny to some of his plans of happy life, and John and Louis believe they are more than kindly remembered by two of those bright girls known as the C. C. of C. C.

Here we may leave Uncle Jeremiah and family to the good of domestic contentment and to the well-earned peace of having lived life well. If the Exposition has awakened the sentiments of patriotism and reverence in the minds of all its visitors, and has broadened their views concerning mankind, and made more charitable their hearts toward the rest of the world, as it has done with this one true rural family, then it has been a mighty success, though millions of dollars were lost in its construction.

This need be none the less true to all, though no two people have seen the same World's Columbian Exposition. In all the vast throngs that have walked its streets and crowded its palaces for half a year there can be no two individuals who have the same story to tell, or who have the same thought to pay out to the world from that mint of human intelligence.

There is so much within the great "White City" that single pieces are lost like flowers in a landscape or like ferns on a mountain side. But its beauties inspire every soul; its refinements chasten every heart; its achievements exalt every mind, and its lessons give strength to every life.

## THE END

Lector House believes that a society develops through a two-fold approach of continuous learning and adaptation, which is derived from the study of classic literary works spread across the historic timeline of literature records. Therefore, we aim at reviving, repairing and redeveloping all those inaccessible or damaged but historically as well as culturally important literature across subjects so that the future generations may have an opportunity to study and learn from past works to embark upon a journey of creating a better future.

This book is a result of an effort made by Lector House towards making a contribution to the preservation and repair of original ancient works which might hold historical significance to the approach of continuous learning across subjects.

**HAPPY READING & LEARNING!**

**LECTOR HOUSE LLP**
**E-MAIL:** lectorpublishing@gmail.com